CHASING WIND

CHASING WIND

A NOVELLA

BY DARA ALSTON

Published by Inkwell Publishing
© 2021 Dara Alston

Scriptures are taken from the HOLY BIBLE, NEW LIVING TRANSLATION, Copyright© 1996, 2004, 2007 by Tyndale House Foundation. Used by permission of Tyndale House Publishers, Inc., Carol Stream, Illinois 60188. All rights reserved. Used by permission.

This is a work of fiction. Names, characters, places, and incidents either are the product of the author's imagination or are used fictitiously. Any resemblance to actual persons, living or dead, events, or locales is entirely coincidental.

All rights reserved. No portion of this book may be reproduced in any for without permission from the publisher, except as permitted by U.S. copyright law.

For permissions, contact dara@ave89co.com

ISBN: 9798766561644

Other titles by Dara Alston:
Inhale
Moon Talks

To the 19-year-old Dara:
you are enough.

PART ONE

"Then I observed that most people are motivated to success because they envy their neighbors. But this too is meaningless—like chasing wind."

—ECCLESIASTES 4:4

CHAPTER ONE

NOVEMBER 1ST

I hate my life.

I know that sounds harsh, but it's true. I just wish things went differently than—

"Hello, Welcome to Butcher & Singer. How can I help you?"

"Baxter, reservation for four please?"

Smoothing down my black pants, I grab the menus and show them to their table.

The father, in his three-piece, gray business suit, pulls out the seat for the mother wearing a white dress that I think I saw while watching the Chanel fashion show on YouTube. The two J. Crew models, who I assume are their kids, sit down next to each parent and look at the menu ... with probably no care in the world.

And here I am, three years after graduating college, working in a restaurant as a hostess. Life is grand.

Walking back to the hostess stand, I hear someone call my name.

"Sydney!"

I turn around to see our newly-hired general manager, Veronica Fedley.

"Ms. Humphries, I cut you from the schedule tomorrow."

"What?" Guests within the restaurant turn their heads. With my hands on my hips and preparing to do my strongest whispering, I say, "Veronica, I've been getting cut from my shifts a lot. Isn't there anyone else you can cut for tomorrow? I really need as many shifts as I can get right now."

"Listen, Sydney, we're anticipating a slow day, so we don't need all of our hostesses. Use it as a rest day." She pats my shoulder and walks off.

With all of the schedule changes I've been receiving, the rent for this month took me for almost everything, and now my shift is being taken from me again. Looking back at the family I just sat, I get lost in a daydream of what it must be like to be a part of that family. I imagine being at the restaurant with both parents, alive, and having a sibling to share it with. I place my linen napkin on my lap and my elbows on the linen tablecloth, comforted by the softness it brings. I'm excited to eat because right after this, I'm going to the Broadway show in town that I've always wanted to see.

Yeah, that would be something.

My daydreaming has come to my aid as I discover I've dreamt the rest of my shift away. As I go to clock out for the day, I feel my phone buzz in my pocket.

"Humphries, are you off of work yet?" my best friend says loudly through the phone.

"Hey, Sydney, how are you? How was your day? My day was fine, thank you for asking—" I say as I roll my eyes. No matter how old Corey and I get, he'll never answer the phone by saying hello.

"Fine. Hello Sydney, how are you?"

"I'm doing well, Corey, thank you, and how are you doing?" I say as I smile, knowing he's probably rolling his eyes on the other end of the line.

"We're at Seventeenth and Market in front of Liberty Place. Come meet us." *Click.*

A normal conversation between one of my best friends and me. Straight, no chaser.

I hightail it the five blocks it takes to get from Fifteenth and Walnut to Seventeenth and Market. *Whew, I need to hit the gym more.* One block in Center City Philadelphia could equate to two or three suburban blocks. I actually don't know if that's true, but I feel like it should be. Bobbing and weaving between people in puffy coats and hoodies, I see Corey's blue Ford pickup truck with its hazard lights on. I get into the back seat and close my eyes as I listen to his twin sister, Carina, in the front seat talking on the phone in Spanish.

These two are *my* family, and I love it, although, I wouldn't mind being adopted by that last family I sat before my shift was over.

I'm jolted awake by Corey pushing hard on the brakes in front of our apartment building. He laughs in the rearview mirror as he puts the car in park.

"You fall asleep every time," he says with a smile.

He's been pulling this prank on me ever since he was sixteen when he first got his driver's license. He was the first one of the three of us to get our license. Rolling my eyes, I let out an exasperated sigh and realize we've made it to our apartment.

Carina goes into the building first, stopping at the bank of mailboxes to the left of the stairs.

"Umm, hermanito, when did you start getting your mail delivered here?" Carina asks Corey.

Uh-oh, I know when she uses "hermanito" with Corey, something's not right.

"Could you please stop calling me that?" he says, pursing his lips. "You're only older than me by two and a half minutes."

"And I'll say it again, *hermanito*, when did you start getting your mail delivered here?"

After two flights of stairs, we go to the middle of the hallway where I open the door to the apartment where Carina and I live.

"Ooh, what's this?" Corey snatches a silver envelope out of Carina's hand, and she hits him on the shoulder with the stack of mail.

"C'mon Corey," I say. "Don't get her angry when she's about to cook. I want to be able to taste the love in this recipe. What are we having tonight?"

"I want to try shrimp and chicken empanadas with mashed yucca and a veggie on the side."

My mouth waters at the thought of dinner. Carina has picked up momentum with her food blog and YouTube channel. Her subscriber count grows every week as she tries new recipes from different countries.

"You know, someday we oughta travel to some of these countries that you're cooking from," I say as I try to find a snack in the fridge to hold me over.

"Yeah, all expenses-paid by Corey Gutierrez, number one draft pick of the Philadelphia Eagles." Carina laughs, and she and I come together for a high-five.

No one would know Corey has been newly drafted into the NFL. It's been almost three months, and he's still wearing the same old sweatpants and T-shirt he always wears. Corey would practice almost every day after school in Roxborough, near where my grandmother used to live. He would always come in late for dinner smelling like a zoo and park right in front of the television to watch ESPN. It's still so surreal that he actually *made* it.

Carina and I were crying when he got the phone call, and we cried even more when they called his name from the stage. I don't believe I ever cried as much as I did that night—well, there was one time . . .

"I'm not taking you guys anywhere," he says as he settles into his recliner.

"Um, excuse me . . ." Carina says. "You're basically the third roommate here, and you do nothing but tell us that we need more juice—"

"Which you're out of, by the way." He chuckles as he fiddles with the silver envelope.

He bought the brown clunker of a recliner he's sitting in to make himself feel at home. Carina's already given the man a key, so I don't know how much more he needs to feel like he belongs. What he needs to feel are boundaries. He comes in and out as he pleases. I go to the sofa next to his recliner and look over his shoulder to see what's in the shiny, silver envelope.

"What's that?" I ask, straining my neck for a better view.

"An invitation."

"An invitation to what?"

"Some BarnesLuke Christmas party. I don't think I'm going to go to it though."

My breath becomes short. He couldn't be talking about—

"Corey, let me see that."

He hands me the envelope and invitation and then grabs the remote. The cardstock is velvety smooth as I run my fingers over the embossed lettering. In my hands, I hold an invitation to the most prestigious Christmas event in Philadelphia: the Luke and Barnes Christmas Gala. The who's who of fashion come from all over the country to celebrate the year in style—pun intended.

"Corey, do you realize what this is?" I ask him. "Do you realize that you've just been invited to one of the most prestigious events in all of Philadelphia?"

My voice becomes louder, and my eyes grow wider. Heat is rising to the top of my head, and my mouth is growing dryer by the second.

"Really? I've never heard of it," he says as he stretches his arm from his recliner to get a roll from the bowl sitting on the dining table. He stuffs it into his mouth, and Carina immediately hits him with the dishcloth she just dried her hands on.

"Hey! Stop eating the food before I make it! Or dinner really will be on you."

Corey rolls his eyes and surfs channels on the television.

"Corey, you cannot be serious right now," I yell. "This isn't some random kid's birthday party. This is the Luke and Barnes annual Christmas gala. Face it, Corey, as the hotshot rookie of the draft, you're popular now. Dare I say it—"

"Don't you say it!"

"A celebrity."

Carina chuckles as she stands over the sizzling pan that's wafting good smells from the kitchen.

I wonder how long dinner will take. I head to the kitchen cabinet for the box of popcorn and put one of the packages in the microwave.

"You know I hate that word!" Corey yells.

"She's right, Corey," Carina says.

I smile like a sister who just told on her older brother and is watching him get in trouble. My friend has no clue.

"I don't know who BarnesLuke is—"

"Luke *and* Barnes!"

"*Excuse* me Miss Fancy Pants. How do you even know about these people?"

I need new friends. Have they not been listening to me for the past fifteen plus years that we've been together? I remember seeing all the cars lined up in front of the Art Museum when I was a child, people taking pictures at the Rocky steps, gowns blowing in the wind, women on the arms of gentleman dressed in tuxedos. From that moment on, I told myself, *I need to be there.* And now I'm holding the only opportunity I probably will ever get to do so in my hands.

"Cor, why don't you just take Syd and make a day of it? You know she likes the fancy stuff."

Corey managed to stuff another roll in the back of his cheek like a chipmunk. "I know *she* likes those things, but I don't. I'm not into all of the bougie stuff."

"Yeah, Carina," I jump in, "Corey would lose his mind with all the place settings and formalities and suits, oh my!" I laugh at my own joke while the room fills only with the sounds of the frying pan.

"Are you saying I can't go to one of those ritzy-ditzy parties and act all—ritzy-ditzy?" Corey puts his recliner back up and faces me.

"You wouldn't even last an hour."

"Are you challenging me, Humphries? Because you know better than anybody that Corey Gutierrez doesn't back down from a challenge."

"Oh no. He spoke of himself in the third person." Carina sighs as she puts some empanadas in a serving dish.

"Yes, I did speak about myself in the third person, and you know what? I'll RSVP to this little party, and you're coming with me, Humphries, as my plus one."

"You *really* think you can make it an entire night with no complaining and no mocking?"

"Of course! In fact, let's make it interesting, If I make it through the entire night with no complaining and no mocking, then . . . you have to cook me dinner for an entire week."

He knows I hate cooking. It's the bane of my existence. The output of energy needed to put a dish together—I'd rather leave it to other people who actually enjoy it. I cross my arms and narrow my eyes.

"Fine. And if I win, you have to wear a suit every day for seven days."

Carina bursts out in laughter. "Oh man, this is going to be interesting. Dinner's ready."

Corey and I go to our circular, wooden dining table and take our seats. Corey prays over the food and immediately shoves what he can in his mouth.

"So, what do you say, Gutierrez? Are you up for the challenge?" I raise an eyebrow as he looks at his sister who looks at the both of us and smiles.

"Challenge accepted."

Corey and Carina talk as I look at the invitation on my right. I run my fingers over it. What was once a dream is now becoming reality.

CHAPTER TWO

NOVEMBER 20TH

So, here I am again with another day off. At least my rent is paid. I lay in my bed and stare at the ceiling for a bit. I don't know what to do today. I don't know how to make this day different from every other day where I would binge-watch Dorian Gray and look for jobs on the internet.

I stare out my window through the empty tree branches at the cars that line the sidewalk. It looks like today will be a nice day. Low fifties with clear skies. With a heavy sigh, I turn around and put my feet to the floor on the gray carpet I keep telling myself I have to vacuum at some point.

My brown bookcase is to my right displaying my

most prized possessions: pictures of Corey, Carina, and I, two of the only pictures I have of my parents, the only picture I have of my grandmother, my high school yearbook, and a few books I keep telling myself I must read—the Bible being one of them.

God and I used to talk every day in college. I can remember praying before tests or talking to Him as I walked to class. He would remind me of what I read in the Bible that morning or that afternoon. I remember praying to God for my internship and then praying for the company to offer me a full-time job—that's all I needed was a full-time job with great pay so I would never have to go back to Philadelphia again. Needless to say, God didn't answer that one. Going back to my home church in Philly when I swore to myself I would never be back here made me resent myself for being such a failure.

I kept myself busy day in and day out looking for jobs in Corporate America when Carina came into my room one day and said, "Listen Syd, the rent has to get paid somehow. Why don't you just get a temporary job for now and keep looking for that corporate position. At least you'll have money coming in."

Enter Butcher & Singer. What was supposed to be a temporary job is now going on three years. I'm now more determined than ever to find my office job, to move from this apartment, to forget any traces that remind me of what I was.

As for church, well, Corey and Carina would never let me hear the end of it if I stopped going. So, I put on my best church smile and say hello to everyone as I go in and out of the building. I also joined one group—the drama group—to make it look like I'm not a complete failure when it comes to my spiritual life.

Now, the drama group is pretty cool. We put on all of the plays for special occasions like Easter and Christmas, and we always manage to squeeze one in for the summer. Honestly, if it weren't for the cool people in the drama group, I know my church experience would be much more miserable than it already is. Not even Carina knows how I've been feeling though, and I want to keep it that way.

"Hey, are you up? Hey, are you up? Hey, are you up?"

I pull my comforter over my head. Carina will not stop knocking until I answer the door. Carina and I are stuck at the hip. We've been that way since we were little. All we had were each other. However, the older I got, the more I realize I need my space. Space to breathe, space to figure out who I am apart from Carina and Corey. I want some time to myself today—a little peace and quiet.

"Yes, come in."

She bursts into the room and pulls the comforter off me.

"C'mon, it's already eight o'clock, and you're just sitting here bumming it."

All of us can't be successful YouTubers, Carina. Sorry to disappoint you.

"It's my day off. This whole day should be a bum fest."

"Look what I found." She hands me a familiar red, white, and silver book—my high school yearbook. Most people would throw their high school yearbook in the trash. Heck, they might even burn it ... but not Carina.

She was voted "Most Likely to Succeed," and I know she would've won Homecoming Queen if Corey didn't win Homecoming King. That would have been awkward.

My life was regularly eclipsed by their accomplishments which made for dark days. I had to make a lane for myself. The only thing I want to remember from high school is the vow I made to myself—make sure I win in the end. We're eight years removed, and I have nothing to show for it. My phone buzzes with a text message from Corey:

Just sent in the RSVP.

The gala! I need money to get a dress for the gala! High school will never repeat itself under my watch.

"I gotta go." I pop up from my bed and prepare to get in the shower.

"Ooh, where are we going?"

"I need to go to Center City for something."

"I can't come?"

"I just want to be by myself for this one." I can tell she's disappointed, but I need to air out my thoughts.

I quickly wash up, get dressed, and make the next bus headed into Center City. The trees that line the Parkway go by fast as I stare out the window. Center City, Philadelphia, is made up of smaller areas that each have its own vibe. I find the newly-opened Parisian café and notice there's a "now hiring" sign in the window.

Walking into the café, I hear French jazz coming through the speakers. Small tables and chairs fill up the space. A long stretch of marble matches the length of the window for customers to sit up high and people watch, a newly found hobby of mine. A young woman with short, blonde hair cut into a pixie brings out a tray of hot croissants that immediately make my mouth water.

"Hi, how can I help you?" Ms. Pixie smiles at me with green eyes and a blinding, white smile. *She must be a model or an actress.*

"Hi. Yes, I saw that you guys were hiring, so I wanted to come in and fill out an application. Oh, and could I also get a croissant?"

"One croissant and application coming right up."

"Thank you."

She smiles as she hands me one of the fresh croissants on a white plate along with a pen and the application. I sit at one of the high-tops so I can look out onto the street. Only one bite of the croissant, and the buttery, flaky goodness is overwhelming. I close my eyes and take in this moment of happiness. The heat and the butter of the croissant melts all my problems away for that moment, and I'm at peace—content. With life. With me.

I open my eyes back to women in high-heels, pencil skirts, sunglasses, and designer bags. There's one in particular who catches my eye. A woman on the sidewalk outside in a bright yellow trench coat comes closer into view. She's wearing black heels with sunglasses that remind me of Audrey Hepburn in "Breakfast at Tiffany's." She's on her cell phone, and she turns into the café.

Stop staring, Sydney!

The door chimes, and she goes straight up to the counter.

"Hi, how can I—"

"Double espresso." Ms. Trenchie shoves a twenty-dollar bill in the waitress's face. Still on her phone, she looks out the window while holding out the bill.

Ms. Pixie takes the bill and goes to make the order.

Sounds like Ms. Trenchie is having a rough day.

"Derek, I don't have time to go to Milan right now. You want me to sign on two new clients."

Milan? She turned down the opportunity to go to Milan?

What I wouldn't give to even *have* the opportunity to go anywhere outside the United States.

Ms. Pixie hands Ms. Trenchie her change, and Trenchie digs in her newly released, black Burberry tote bag and takes out her matching wallet to put in the change. She takes out her wireless earbuds and puts them in her ears as Ms. Pixie returns with her drink. She grabs her espresso with not so much as a thank you and continues her conversation as she walks out of the door. She could be someone who would live at The Atlantic.

I look down at my black slacks paired with white sneakers and a beige turtleneck. Some would say I have a resourceful way of maintaining clothes. My turtleneck has a patch of forest green along the neck because of a wear-and-tear hole that showed up last year. A stray dog who saw my pants leg as breakfast caused the red patch at the bottom cuff of my right leg. This resourceful way of maintaining clothes didn't go over too well in high school. It contributed to one of my nicknames, "Patches." I quickly shake the surfacing memory from my head. It took me so long to recover from all the mental space it stole from me once I graduated high school, and I refuse to let it take any more room.

Ms. Trenchie.

I bet she doesn't have to worry about patches or tears or holes. Her biggest problem right now is probably turning down going to Milan because she's "busy." Oh, how I wish I could be busy doing *something*.

Oh right, the application. I finish filling it out and return it to Ms. Pixie.

"Hold on for just a minute." Ms. Pixie goes to the back and returns with a short, bald man with black-rimmed glasses.

His white, Oxford shirt is untucked, and his khaki pants could use a steam or two, but there's something endearing about his look. I can tell that he takes himself seriously enough to wear an Oxford shirt with khakis, but not too seriously as to where he thinks they need to be ironed.

She points at me and then at my application. I smile as I look around and try to let my right ear hear what they're saying. I think they're speaking French.

"Mademoiselle Humphries?"

Yup. Definitely French.

"Yes," I say with a smile. *Don't ruin this, Sydney. Remember, you need a dress for the gala.*

"Hello, my name is Monsieur Demont. I'm the head pastry chef and owner for the boulangerie."

"It's nice to meet you, Monsieur Demont."

Having watched three French movies, I try my best to pronounce his name exactly the way he does.

"Let's have a seat, mademoiselle."

I follow him to the back of the café to a two-person table in the corner by the window.

"So, I see here that you work for Butcher & Singer."

"Yes, I've worked there for the past three years as a hostess."

"And you like it?"

Uh-oh. Trick question.

"I enjoy engaging with different people of different backgrounds, and I enjoy the food, of course." I say with a chuckle. Ms. Pixie brings me a glass of water, and I take sips from the glass.

"And I see here that you graduated from University of Connecticut?"

"Yes. I got my degree in marketing. I had an internship right when I graduated, but then that didn't work out as intended, so I began working at Butcher & Singer, and it seems. . ." *Sydney! He didn't ask for a life story.* "I'm sorry. Yes, I got my degree in marketing." I take another sip of water and clear my throat, look out at the window and then down at my hands. It's been three years since I've been on an interview, and yet I acted as if it's my first time.

"You know what, mademoiselle? I normally don't do this, but I have a good feeling about you. You are educated, you have food service experience, and you seem like a quick study." He folds his hands together and smiles.

"I am, sir—I'm sorry, monsieur—I am."

"Oui. Well, can you start tomorrow? You can work the opening shift with Tina." He nods with his head in the direction of Ms. Pixie—Tina.

"Monsieur, I'm so grateful. Thank you so much." I shake his hand and wave at Miss Pix—Tina.

"Welcome to the team," she says as she smiles. "Be here by five a.m. tomorrow."

My insides tighten at the time. But I remember the reason why I'm doing this. *The dress.*

"Five a.m. Got it. See you tomorrow!" I say with forced enthusiasm.

I walk out of the boulangerie with my head a little higher than before.

CHAPTER THREE

DECEMBER 3RD

"Frosted windowpanes, candles gleaming inside, painted candy canes on the tree . . ." The radio in the mall is belting out my favorite Christmas carol of all—The Christmas Waltz.

With only one week left before the gala, Corey and I managed to find some free time in our schedules to shop for our outfits. Carina wanted to be surprised and opted out of coming.

Caffeine feels like a necessary decision for this trip, so I head over to Starbucks and secure my Venti Chestnut Praline Latte. Thank the Lord for mobile ordering. The mall is abnormally busy. I know people have to do their Christmas shopping, but this crowd seems like a next-level-Black-Friday type of crowd. I'm trying to get to Clarissa's Boutique, but shopping bags and puffy coats are in my way. I feel like I'm inside the wardrobe but can't quite make it to Narnia.

"Here. It's over here." Corey grabs me and takes me to a suit and tie place he found on the internet called *Suit and Tie*. While I love the Justin Timberlake hit, I don't think this place is going to have what Corey needs to really impress Luke + Barnes.

An older gentleman with a gray, tweed jacket and a measuring tape around his neck comes out from the back.

"Hello, what can I do ya' for?"

"Yes, I'm looking for a suit for a gala," Corey says. He pulls at his collar and looks around the store.

"Ah, you and the pretty little lady got a fancy holiday party coming up, huh?"

"Me and the pretty lady have more so of a holiday party bet that I'm trying to secure a win for, so I need to be as comfortable as possible."

Did Corey just call me pretty?

The older gentleman takes Corey to the fitting rooms, and I grab a seat by the store window. All of the suit jackets are color coordinated and hung along the top racks around the store. From yellow to black, every color in the rainbow and then some are accounted for. The coordinating pants are folded on shelves that line the bottom, and the ties sit in the middle to complete the sandwich.

Corey comes out of the fitting room with a similar gray-tweed jacket as the older gentleman is wearing, a white Oxford shirt, and black pants with black patent-leather shoes. He looks at a cap that is reminiscent of newspaper boys way back in the day and puts it on his head.

"Hey now, I kind of—"

"No," I say.

"What? Why not?"

"Absolutely not. This is not the Great Depression. This is not the 1940's. You're not delivering newspapers. No."

I push him back into the dressing room. *This is going to be harder than I thought. Wait, Corey has the money now, I don't know why I didn't think of this sooner.*

"Corey, get dressed. There's somewhere else we can go. I'll be waiting outside."

I walked outside the store and immediately collide with a man who is on his cell phone. The perpetrator looks back at me to see who he mauled down, and suddenly my life went in slow motion. His glasses frame a face that I only thought existed in the movies.

Is that the "Hallelujah Chorus" I hear in the background?

He keeps walking as I lay on the ground, but his

face lingers in my mind as I am now in the beginning stages of planning our wedding.

"Syd, you okay?" Corey comes over in the middle of the rush. He picks me up by the arm.

I dust off imaginary lint from my pants. "Yeah, I'm fine." My voice trails off as I look in the direction of my future spouse who's long gone now.

"So, you said you know a place where we could go?"

"Oh! Yes. And in fact," I intentionally clear my throat as loudly as I can, "If you would like to get me an early Christmas present, they also sell dresses there that a young lady could wear for such an occasion as this."

"Oh, really?" he asks unamused. "Syd, you took on a second job so you could get the dress you want, didn't you?"

Dang. He got me.

I take a big sigh. "I guess you're right. That was the reason I picked up a second job, *but* you know with all of the shifts that I worked, I still only managed to swing a dress that I could pick up from Macy's *on sale*. I wouldn't be able to compete with the likes of those who'll be at this gala, and you wouldn't want the person on your arm to be wearing any old thing because you know the paparazzi will be there and—"

"Alright!" He says as we walk into the food court. "Alight. Fine. I'll get your dress. But your limit is two hundred dollars and that includes shoes."

"Two hundred dollars? Corey, where we're going, you couldn't even get a tie for two-hundred dollars."

"What? Then why are we going there, Syd? You know I'm not trying to spend money like that." Corey places our usual order at Chic-Fil-A, and we stand to the side to wait.

"Corey, you know as much as I do that you are in the public eye now. You have to be conscious of what you're wearing. More importantly, *who* you're wearing. That's why we're going to go to Luke + Barnes."

* * *

We took an extra twenty-five minutes to find a parking spot because Mr. Bargain didn't want to park in a garage.

"Why pay all of that when I can just walk a couple blocks, get some exercise, and only pay three-fifty?"

I shake my head as Corey pulls into a parking spot five blocks away. Hopefully, cold winds would lift me up and carry me the rest of the way. We arrive at an arched doorway that forced me to look up at about four levels of beige stonework.

A lantern sconce hangs on the wall to my left with brown doors right under the archway. Once we enter, light sounds of jazz came through the speakers. Corey and I both look up and around. Out of all of my years loving this brand, I've never stepped foot inside of the store. I would always think I'm too underdressed.

Judging by what I'm wearing now, I have reason to still feel that way. I have on some skinny blue jeans, white sneakers, and a black puffer jacket. Corey has on his daily uniform—black track suit with black sneakers. Yep, we are severely underdressed.

To my left are mannequins dressed in navy blue and black suits lined up across the wall that leads to a staircase. A guy comes from the back in a dark-gray, pen-striped suit, with a white shirt and red tie.

"Hello. Welcome to Luke and Barnes. Do you have an appointment?"

Whoa. His cologne reaches us before he does. This dude *smells* expensive. Like a newly discovered tax bracket of expensive. His face forms a bit of a smile the closer he gets. Each step is deliberate. The dark curls on his head are pulled in every direction, like a guy's version of the perfect messy bun. I'm both captivated and embarrassed as I remember the horror that is under my coat. I peek down to make sure my coat is zipped up all the way. There's no need to scare Mr. Platinum with my boring, old, worn-out clothes.

"We don't have an appointment. She brought me here because we're going to the Christmas gala, and I need a suit."

Straight, no chaser.

"You two will be going to the gala?" Mr. Platinum looks shocked as he tries to hold back his laughter.

Then a look of recognition comes on his face. "Wait, I've seen you before." Mr. Platinum points at Corey.

And so it begins.

"You're Corey Gutierrez, aren't you?"

And at that moment, a conversation began that reminded me of watching a tennis match in the sky. My head goes back and forth as these two tall men talk to each other. Stats, names, and contract payouts, among other things, are topics that each result with Corey putting his head down and saying, "Aw, thanks man. You know, I just do what I can."

"It's a shame you guys didn't make it to the playoffs this year," Mr. Platinum says.

Corey looks around the store. He's never been one to enjoy being the center of attention. Sure, he'll make a couple jokes on his birthday about the rest of us being peasants, in which case Carina and I would gang up on him for a pillow fight, but at the core, he truly loves the game of football.

The door opens, and a familiar combination of bun, coat, and heels walks towards us.

Ms. Trenchie.

She takes off her sunglasses to reveal light-brown eyes ringed by long, eyelashes.

I pull at my coat again.

"Olivia, we have a celebrity in the showroom," Mr. Platinum says to Ms. Trenchie.

Showroom? Once you get into a different tax bracket, I guess stores turn into showrooms.

"And who do we have here?" Her face goes into a soft smile. Completely opposite of what I witnessed a few weeks ago. And her voice sounds like a red-velvet carpet. Like she should be a radio DJ for a smooth jazz station. *She wasn't talking like that at the café.*

"Corey Gutierrez." Corey says as he puts his hand out and smiles with a bit more confidence than he had thirty seconds ago.

Wait a minute.

"Olivia McMillan." She receives his handshake with a smile.

Olivia McMillan. McMillan. McMillan!

"Wait, are you related to Steve McMillan?" I ask.

"Is there anything that I can help you with, Corey?" She says as she moves closer to him and almost in front of me. Steve McMillan is one of the biggest real-estate developers in the city. He owns a lot of the buildings throughout Center City.

"My friend Sydney and I are going to be at your Christmas gala."

"Oh, you're coming to the gala?" she asks.

"Yeah. My friend Sydney and I," he responds.

Thanks for trying to include me, Corey.

"Who?" she asks looking from left to right.

I clear my throat and offer my hand. "Sydney." I feel all of my insides working together to force a smile across my face. She turns around and quickly looks me up and down.

"Actually, Olivia, I was helping Corey," Mr. Platinum says a little too eagerly. "I know you have lots of paperwork and meetings and such. I'll handle this, and you can just head on upstairs."

"Tristan, make sure you take good care of our guest. No request is too big, and I look forward to seeing you at the gala, Mr. Gutierrez. Oh, and nice meeting you, Cindy."

Corey smiles and watches her as she walks to the back of the room and gets on the elevator. My insides grow tighter as they wave at each other.

"It's ... Sydney!"

The doors of the elevator have already closed, and I see Mr. Plat—Tristan—quickly roll his eyes.

Hmmm.

Now that I know Ms. Trench—Olivia—is going to be at the gala, I need to make sure my dress is perfect. But I need to focus on Corey's suit first. Tristan takes Corey and me upstairs to the second floor where there are suits hung along the walls like paintings in an art museum. The marble flooring continues from the first floor, and there's a table with a computer and a guest chair. Spotlights highlight navy, black, and gray suits that each have a small, white plaque under them.

"Ms. Sydney, you can wait right here while I get Mr. Gutierrez set up in our fitting area."

The fitting area consists of three mirrors configured like a tri-fold poster board with a circular podium in the middle. There are three doors for individual dressing rooms on the right. As Corey is in one dressing room, I busy myself looking at the information on the plaques along the wall, all the while thinking about Olivia and Corey. The way his eyes lingered as she walked away, the way she smiled at him. Ugh, it all makes me sick!

Then why can't you stop thinking about it?

"I don't know!" I whine.

Oh wow; I said that out loud. I'm praying no one heard me. I really have to work on keeping my thoughts inside of my head sometimes. But now I'm starting to think about why thinking about them makes me sick on top of why I can't stop thinking about them together. I close my eyes and think about the croissants I had at the French café. What I wouldn't give to have one of them right now.

"So, what do you think?" Corey asks.

I turn around to see Corey facing the mirror in a black tuxedo with cummerbund and bow tie.

He messes with the button on the cuff of each sleeve and puts his hand in his right pocket to make a pose. He laughs and turns around to me.

"Why are you so quiet? What do you think?" He looks down at his pants and fiddles with the button on the jacket while Tristan takes his measurements.

Yeah, I've seen him in a suit before. He wore one for prom and then for graduation, and for my grandmother's funeral ... oh, and for the draft. But there's something about this suit, this moment, seeing Corey laugh, play around and look—comfortable. What is this feeling in my stomach?

Make it stop!

"Humphries!" Corey waves a hand that breaks my current dream sequence.

"Huh? What? Oh yeah. You look alright. You look great. Fantastic. I mean, yeah. Just great."

"And what don't you know?" he asks me.

"What are you talking about?"

"I heard you yell 'I don't know.' Were you on the phone with someone?"

He heard me!

"Never mind that. Let's see what the other suit looks like."

I quickly turn around and begin to brush imaginary lint from my jeans thinking that it will brush away the flutters that are in my stomach. *Don't acknowledge the flutters. Don't acknowledge the flutters.* I walk a little further back from the fitting area to find a plaque to busy my mind.

"Humphries, what about this one?" Corey asks.

"Yep, you look great."

"You're not even looking."

"Yep. You're great."

"Syd, c'mon."

It's not often he uses a variation of my first name. And for some reason, it feels different this time. I turn around, and there he is, holding both arms out with a boyish grin on his face. He looks so unsure of himself. He's in a gray tuxedo with black lapels with the same shirt and bow tie. Instead of a cummerbund, he's wearing a matching vest.

"Yeah, you look great."

"Would you stop playing and come over here? I want you to see the suit."

"Yeah, I can see it great from right here." *I need a glass of water.*

"Sydney."

My teeth clench immediately when he says my name. I walk closer—slowly—but I eventually get there. I look up at his face as he's searching mine to get my opinion.

"What do you think? Honestly."

"Honestly?"

"Honestly."

"Corey, you look fantastic." I pull together a smile that doesn't look too forced. Since when were his eyes gray? And since when did he have such a nice smile? I back away slowly as Tristan comes out.

"Tristan, is there any water I can have?"

"Absolutely, Ms. Sydney. Give me a moment."

Corey turns back around to look at himself in the mirror, playing with his cuffs.

Tristan comes back out with a chilled, glass bottle of water and hands it to me.

"I think I'm going to go with the classic, black tuxedo, Tristan."

"You don't want to try the third one on?" I ask.

"This is my first gala. I don't even have a classic black tux. I think that one is cool."

"Traditional tuxedo it is." Tristan says as he grabs the suit from the dressing room and points us in the direction of the table. Tristan sits in a chair behind a large computer screen.

"Alright Mr—"

"You can just call me Corey."

"Corey. Your total, including tailoring, comes to $2,500."

"$2,500?" Corey says in a voice loud enough for the whole store to hear. "Who made this suit? Jesus?"

I dip my head low as I take a sip from my water bottle.

"The gala is next week, and we have to find time to squeeze in another fitting after the suit is tailored to make sure everything is perfect." Tristan says.

Corey sits back in his chair with a look of defeat, and then he looks at me.

"If my suit costs that much, how are you going to get your dress?"

We sit there quietly.

"I'll give you two a moment," Tristan says as he stands up.

"No, you don't have to do that, Tristan." Corey says, looking defeated. "I'll get the suit. And keep my card on file so Sydney can get a dress."

Tristan types on his computer and prints out a paper receipt that he hands to Corey.

"You go ahead and get your dress. I'll be in the car." Corey gets up from the chair and heads downstairs.

"Would you prefer to walk up the stairs or take the elevator?" Tristan asks.

"We can take the stairs."

"Seems like you have a really good friend, Ms. Sydney."

"I do, Tristan. I do."

CHAPTER FOUR

DECEMBER 10TH

It's the day of the Christmas gala, and my stomach is in my throat. Butcher & Singer has been on the back burner as I've been getting less and less shifts which made me take more shifts at the cafe. Corey and Carina hated it. I barely saw them and barely had time to go to Bible Study and Sunday service, which I didn't mind, and I had a reasonable excuse—work. Today, I took an opening shift so that I can get off early to prepare for the gala.

Corey: I'll be there at 4:30

The gala's cocktail hour starts at five p.m., which Corey wasn't originally going to go to, but Carina convinced him by telling him it would be good for his image and his brand to be there early to mingle and get to know people.

Of course, I wanted the opportunity to savor as much of this moment as I could. I got a decent enough dress, but nothing close to the dress I wanted because I needed to be mindful of how much I was spending since this was on Corey's dime. He rarely talked to me for two days after we went shopping until Carina forced us into our living room to talk it out.

"Sydney, I'm just not into this stuff as much as you are. I really don't care about how expensive my suit is or who I'm wearing."

"You're complaining already, and we haven't even stepped foot into the gala."

"I'm not complaining; I'm just saying why should I have to worry about this stuff when I'm probably not going to see these people ever again."

"I'll bet you'll see Olivia again."

"Oh, shut up," he said.

"And who's Olivia?" Carina said, crossing her arms.

"I'll see you at the gala." Corey gets up and walks out the door. And that was two days ago. To the outside world, two days is nothing. But for three friends who spend almost every waking minute with each other, two days may as well have been two months.

I look at my dress hanging on the back of my bedroom door. I haven't seen it or unwrapped it since

I came home with it. Pulling it down, I lay it on my bed and stare at it. The richness of the red brings such a perfect nod to the season we're celebrating. My fingers run across the sweetheart neckline and all the way down the satin, floor-length gown. I'm excited to see how the gold jewelry I picked up from Macy's pairs with this strapless dress.

I wonder what Olivia is going to wear.

Between washing and detangling my hair and doing my make-up, I look at my phone to see that it's almost four-thirty p.m. I give myself a once-over in the mirror behind my door. I never thought I'd be standing here about to go to the gala I've dreamed about since I was a child. I'll be among those with the flowing gowns and shiny jewels. I look behind me at the train of my gown and smile. *This is my moment.*

I walk out my door and hear Carina screaming into her phone with her back to me.

"Corey where the heck are you? You were supposed to be here by four-thirty. Sydney's in the room getting dressed, and you haven't even gotten in your tux yet. What in the world is wrong? A bow tie? You're late because of a stupid bow tie?"

"Tell him I'll help him with it when he gets here," I say softly and sadly. Maybe the cocktail hour isn't all that important anyway, right?

"Sydney!" Carina says as she immediately ends the call and walks closer. Her mouth is open, and her arms are out for a hug. "Oh, my goodness, you look so beautiful. Oh Sydney! Let me take a picture."

I straighten up and put on a smile that I hope could fool her. Mission failed.

"Syd, what's wrong? Everything's going to go right. I promise. This is going to be one of the best nights of your life."

I want to believe her, but the way my life is set up, nothing ever goes as planned.

Thirty minutes later, Corey arrives with his shirt untucked and bow tie laying around his neck.

Carina looks at me, looks at Corey, and walks into the kitchen.

Corey walks toward me and looks at me…almost like he was looking at Olivia, but this look is different. It looks like he wants to say something. God knows I want to say something, but my brain is firing off so many thoughts, I don't know which one to take. I break eye contact and walk up to him as he's tucking in his shirt.

"Hello," I say. I grab the two ends of the bow tie and proceed to tie it around his neck. The flutters decide to make an appearance, and I don't understand why. I've been close to Corey before. But just like in Luke + Barnes when I saw him in his suit, this time is different. Hints of cinnamon spice and oak waft to my nose. He's wearing cologne!

He knows I love cinnamon.

I close my eyes for a brief moment, taking in the scent, and I feel the flutters in my stomach increase along with my heart rate.

"Hi," he responds.

His eyes are still on me. I can feel it.

I clear my throat as I make sure his tie is straight and then back up to look at him. To look at my best friend who is in a tuxedo about to take me to the gala of my dreams. To look at Corey who bought a suit that he would never have otherwise, and on top of that, paid for my dress.

"I got you something," I say as I give him a silver box with a silver ribbon wrapped around it. "It's something for tonight."

He looks at me, then at the box, then back at me with a smile of curiosity. He opens the box and finds two silver cufflinks with a small "c" etched in each one.

"Sydney."

The butterflies evolve into dragonflies as I put one hand over my stomach and smile.

"Could you help me put them on?" he asks.

"Um, yeah. Sure."

I walk up and take one of the cufflinks out of the box. As I'm putting one in, a loud crunch of chips comes from the kitchen. Corey and I both look at Carina.

"Y'all are so cute," she says as she smiles like a mom sending her kid off to prom. "I want to take a picture; hold on."

I rush and put the second cuff link in, and Corey and I share one more look at each other. This will for sure be a very interesting night.

* * *

We pull up to the steps of the Art Museum, but instead of going to the front with the Rocky steps, we go to the West entrance where we're met by a parking attendant.

"Are you here for the Luke and Barnes gala?"

"Yes, sir."

"Names, please."

Corey tells the attendant our names as another attendant opens my door. Corey gives a small smile, offers me his arm, and I take it as we walk up the steps. Entering the museum, Corey gives our names again, and he takes us to the ballroom.

We pass by the tallest Christmas tree I've ever seen. It stands almost as tall as the museum itself with red leaves and gold ornaments shining from every direction. Red and gold presents of all different sizes are stacked neatly under the tree. I guess I fit in more than I thought I would.

"Enjoy, Sir and Ma'am. You're going to be dining at table four this evening."

The usher smiles and moves away from the door to show a dimly lit room filled with dazzling ball gowns swaying on the floor. A jazz band in a corner to my left is softly playing "Angels We Have Heard on High."

"You wanna look for our table?" Corey asks.

"Sure."

As we walk across the ballroom, people begin to whisper to each other as they point at us. I locked eyes with a few couples and put on a strained smile in hopes that we could get to our table before I have to accidentally lock eyes with anyone else. We find our table on the front row on the other side of the room.

Sitting down, I must look up to see the enormous, silver chandeliers hanging from the ceiling. Light catches certain jewels that make the chandelier sparkle differently every time I look at it. I look at the place card for the seat next to me: Nicholas Spencer.

That name sounds like money.

"What are all of these forks for?" Corey whispers.

"Each fork is for a different course, a different type of meal."

"And these knives?"

"Same thing."

"Same thing with the cups, too?"

"Mm hmm."

"Which one is mine?"

"All of your glasses, knives, and spoons are on

your right side, and all of your forks are on the left. Desert utensils are at the top."

"How do you know all of this?"

"I read."

"So, you're saying I don't read?" he says as he playfully elbows me

"You said it; I didn't." I smile as a server comes to pour water into our glasses.

I guzzle the water down as soon as the server leaves.

"What are you nervous about?" Corey asks.

"What are you talking about?" I respond, knowing exactly what he's talking about. I just don't like that he had to say it out loud.

"You always drink a lot of water when you're nervous."

"No, I don't," I say as I motion for the server to come back to our table with more water.

"Humphries, you forget who you're talking to. I was with you back in high school when you thought you had a date with this guy you liked, and he never showed."

"I don't know what you're talking about." *Can that server walk any slower?*

"And the time you were opening your acceptance letter from UCONN—"

"Yep, doesn't ring a bell." *A snail could have gotten to me faster than this server.*

"And when I was trying on those suits at Luke and Barnes …"

My eyes go wide, and I grab my water glass. *I'll just meet the server halfway.* I don't know why God decided to make me this way, but it's true. My throat becomes the Sahara Desert, and I'm in need of all the water the Atlantic Ocean can offer. I drink the water on the opposite side of the ballroom, but I'm not alone for long.

"Now what is a beautiful woman like yourself doing standing here by herself?"

My glass doesn't leave my mouth as I look to see the same face that has been in my dreams since he knocked me down in the mall. His hair is slicked back into a bun at the top of his neck. He has on a gray tuxedo with a white shirt, black bow-tie and cummerbund to match. I look around, and he's the only one wearing gray tonight. He rubs the stubble of his beard a couple times before putting his hand in his pocket.

"Nicholas Spencer."

He holds out his other hand, and I slowly swallow what little water was in my mouth. *Help me Jesus.* He's the one who's going to be sitting next to me. I smile as I take another drink. Within seconds I see a figure come into view.

"Hey Sydney, who's this?"

Corey stands close behind me, and I regret taking that last gulp as I now look at an empty water glass.

"Hey, I know you. You're Corey Gutierrez. Man, it's a shame you guys didn't make it to the playoffs."

"Um, excuse me," I say to a server walking by. I match their pace and then head over to the table to sit down. *But wait, they're sitting here too*. I've should've thought this plan through.

Corey walks over, fiddling with the buttons of his jacket as Mr. Slickb—Nicholas—went somewhere else.

"Who was that?" Corey asks in a defensive tone.

"His name is Nicholas Spencer."

"You know him from somewhere?"

"I just met him tonight, Corey. What is this; are you the FBI or something?"

I gulp my last of the fourth glass of water and immediately feel all four glasses coming into my bladder.

"I'll be back," I say as I pull up my dress to my ankles. I actually don't know where the bathroom is, but I'm not going to let anyone else know that. It's a shame that I've lived in Philadelphia my whole life and not have once stepped foot into the Art Museum. I go to the left because in my movie watching experience, restrooms are always to the left. Little did I know I would be walking right back outside.

Right it is then.

I head to the restroom and where I thought it would be like the bathroom of a seventeenth century Italian mansion, it reminds me of the restrooms we had in high school.

I stop to look in a mirror. "Sydney, you can do this. This is the night you've been dreaming of. Make it a night that you'll never forget. Go back in there and own the room. Don't be just 'Sydney.' Be Sydney Jamillah Humphries, woman of mystery and intrigue that captures everyone's attention. SJH. SJH."

But first, go to the bathroom before you ruin your dress.

I walk out of the restroom no longer just Sydney, but Sydney Jamillah Humphries. My head is held a little bit higher, and I meet people's gaze with a smile as I walk back into the ballroom. I get to my seat just in time because Mr. Barnes—Mr. Derek Barnes—is taking the microphone to speak.

"Excuse me. Can I have everyone's attention please?"

The room quiets down, and the band plays softer as Mr. Barnes waves for people to come in. His salt-and-pepper hair is flicked up into such a perfect wave that the ocean would be jealous. He's in a navy-blue tuxedo with black lapels and a black bow-tie.

Nicholas takes his seat next to me and smiles as he sits down. I happen to turn my head to Corey whose eyes are boring lasers at Nicholas.

I need a refill of water.

With one hand in his pocket, Mr. Barnes holds the microphone and continues to speak.

"Good evening, everyone, and merry Christmas."

"Merry Christmas," everyone says in unison.

"Merry Christmas," Corey says after the room was already quiet.

I look at him, and he shrugs as he mouths *What?* Like he doesn't know what he did wrong.

I shake my head and turn my attention back to Mr. Barnes.

"It's that time of the year again. It's time to celebrate another great year that has gone by with old friends, and hopefully leave with new ones. We're going to get started with dinner. The servers are going to come to your table and ask your preference of dish, and after that feel free to mingle; the dance floor is open all evening. We paid good money for this room, so make sure the dance floor gets some good use this year, huh?"

Chuckles break out in different pockets of the room.

"I want to make sure everyone enjoys themselves and enjoys the holiday. Merry Christmas, everyone!"

"Merry Christmas!" The room says in unison.

"Merry Christmas," Corey says seconds after everyone else.

I look at him and shake my head as the server comes over to fill my water glass.

An angel, indeed.

"So, Sydney, what brings you to the gala?" Nicholas says.

"She's here with me," Corey pipes up—a little too loudly I might add.

"Okay," Nicholas says, chuckling with a slight roll of the eyes. "I'm sure Sydney could've said that herself."

I close my lips together as tightly as I can to wish myself away.

Can I really click my heels three times? Wait, remember, SJH. SJH.

"Well, Nicholas, Corey's right. I'm here with him as his plus one."

"Well, I hope that won't stop you from dancing with me at some point this evening."

"I don't think it will."

"Um—" Corey interjects.

"And what will you be having tonight, sir?"

Saved by the server.

"I think Sydney will be just fine dancing with me," Corey says after the servers take our order.

"I think Sydney is able to think for herself and dance with whoever she chooses." *Wait, I just talked about myself in the third person.*

"Why did you just talk about yourself in the third person?" Corey asks.

"I don't know. Either way," I turn to Nicholas, "I'll definitely be able to dance with you tonight. I look forward to it."

"So do I," Nicholas says as he stands up to button his tuxedo jacket. "If you'll excuse me, I'm going to do some of that mingling Mr. Barnes talked about."

He smiles and then stands for a moment. It looks like he's thinking of asking me a question, but he isn't completely sure. "Sydney, would you like to come with me?"

"What?" Corey says.

"I would love to."

"What?" Corey says again.

Nicholas offers his arm, and I gladly take it. I don't have time to give lessons on formal dinnerware or have close calls of embarrassment every five minutes. I walk with Nicholas, and he introduces me to old millionaires and new millionaires, classic fashion icons, and up-and-coming sensations. There was one person I was hoping to avoid tonight but—

"Olivia," Nicholas says, "meet Sydney. Sydney, this is Olivia McMillan. She's second in command for Mr. Barnes."

Mr. Barnes? So, the Derek that she was talking to on the phone that day in the café was Mr. Derek Barnes? *Oh, my goodness.* Olivia looks gorgeous in an emerald green gown that has lace interwoven with satin. *But you look alright, too Sydney.*

"We've met already. It's nice to see you again, Olivia." My stomach is hurting the entire time I say it, but I managed to get it out.

"We have?" she asks.

I look down momentarily at the floor as if my thoughts fell out my imaginary pocket.

"I understand you don't remember, what, with you

captivated by Corey. He's sitting right over there if you want to talk to him."

She quickly looks me up and down and turns to Nicholas. "And how do you know Silvy?"

"It's Sydney," I say.

"We actually just met tonight."

"Did you?" she says, an amused smile playing at her lips.

"Well, we can't have Mr. Gutierrez sitting by himself now, can we?"

"He's not, I'm sitting next him," I say.

"Right, as you stand here with Nicholas. You all have a good evening." Her dress moves in sync with her sway as she walks toward Corey.

"Well, I think that gives us our cue to dance, don't you think?" Nicholas looks at me and smiles out of the side of his mouth.

"I think so." I lean my head to the side and smile.

And he dances. Nicholas is no stranger to a ballroom. We take a formal stance, and he turns me across the entire dance floor, or so it seems. It feels like the train of my dress is filling up the entire floor as I spin. We're the only ones on the dance floor, that is, until I feel a little hand on my dress. I look down and see a little girl with black and green ribbons wrapped around her blonde pigtails. Her green dress is covered with a little black jacket that has a bow in the center of her neck.

"Excuse me," she says as she gently taps me. "I really like your dress. Are you a princess?"

"Aww," I laugh and bend down to meet her. "I am not a princess, but I'm sure you are. And thank you for liking my dress. What's your name?"

"Sophia."

"Sophia, I'm Sydney."

"I'm four!" she says.

"Wow, you are a big girl."

"I am! And I have a doll, her name is Christy!"

Sophia turns and runs towards the tables, her pigtails jumping up and down.

"Seems like you made a new friend," Nicholas says as he grabs my hand. He puts my hand on the top of his shoulder as he grabs my waist. The band slows down to the tune of "Have Yourself a Merry Little Christmas." Heat rushes to my cheeks, and I look down as we softly sway back and forth. I replay the conversation—or lack thereof—I had with Olivia earlier. Maybe Sydney Jamillah Humphries came on too strong?

"What are you thinking about?" Nicholas asks.

But before I can answer, I feel a familiar tug on the bottom of my dress. I turn around and see Sophia holding up a barbie doll with a blue ball gown. Mouthing "sorry" to Nicholas, I stoop down and grab Sophia's doll.

"She's so pretty." I say, turning the doll around.

"She's my favorite."

"Yeah?"

"I have another one, too! C'mon!" Sophia grabs my hand, and I stand up and follow behind her trotting pace.

I turn back to Nicholas who is smiling as his head drops. He slowly follows behind. But we don't go that far because we are right at...

"Oh, Mr. Barnes" I say.

"Sophia, are you making friends?" Mr. Barnes smiles at me. "I'm sorry."

"No, it's no problem at all. It's a pleasure to meet you, Mr. Barnes. I'm Sydney." I extend my hand, and Mr. Barnes shakes it, introducing me to his wife and daughter. Uh oh, I feel the Sahara Desert coming.

"She's a princess, Grandpa!" Sophia says as she grabs her other doll. I laugh and brush down imaginary lint from my dress. *The* Derek Barnes is inches away from me, and I've been talking to his granddaughter. I manage to make eye contact with a server.

"Excuse me, could I have some water?"

"Grandpa, can she sit with us?"

"Well, sweetheart—"

"This is actually my seat," Olivia says as she sits down in front of me. Corey is right next to her with both hands in his pockets. I give him a "what are you doing" look.

— 51 —

"Derek, this is Mr. Corey Gutierrez, the newest draft pick for the Eagles," Olivia says.

"But Grandpa—" Sophia screams.

"Sophia, Ms. Sydney can't sit with us right now, okay? That's Ms. Olivia's seat."

"But I don't like Ms. Olivia." Sophia crosses her arms and gives a frown that rivals the likes of Shirley Temple.

Laughing seems to be inappropriate at the moment, but what can you do when a kid tells the truth? Oh, to be like Sophia and not care what people think and not hold back on my feelings or thoughts. Corey and Nicholas are standing behind me, and I look at both of them—void of thought or feeling. My ear catches on to what Mr. Barnes is talking to his wife about. *A new line of menswear?* No teeth show as I smile at Corey and Nicholas. I really want to hear what Mr. Barnes is saying.

"I think having the menswear collection inspired by the city—the skyscrapers, the modernity, the industrious nature of a hustling, bustling downtown. Think about it: grays, hues of blues, shades of white. Think about the campaign shoots behind it. Robust amounts of silver and titanium watches coupled with cuff links and ties and—"

"Oh, that is a wonderful idea, Mr. Barnes!" I say. I couldn't help myself. The entire table looks at me.

"I like Princess Sydney, Grandpa!"

I smile and nervously laugh as I put my hands behind my back, grabbing hold of my hands for dear life.

"I really do think it's a wonderful concept. It's almost like a regeneration of the Renaissance concept you had a few years ago. Except this would be Millennium Renaissance man. You could even make callbacks to the previous collection with small hints of red in the handkerchiefs or neckties," I add.

Mr. Barnes turns around with a smile of surprise on his face.

"You know about the Renaissance collection?" he asks.

Olivia's gaze shifts between Mr. Barnes and me.

"Oh, yes sir. That was the collection that I did a case study on for one of my business classes. I have my marketing degree from UCONN." I nervously clear my throat and smile as I look at him and his wife. *He didn't ask for all of that information, Sydney. Calm down.*

"I think contrasting the textures of metal and fabric would make for a strong concept and collection for the new year," I add. Turning to my left, I softly pull Corey closer. "Corey here is wearing one of your traditional tuxedos that's a wool blend, and even though these cuff links are nickel, they make a bright, contrasting statement for the suit. It would be a great companion to a watch as well." I lift up Corey's sleeve, but there's no watch to be found, so I just lightly tap his wrist and smile. *I think it's time for some water.*

Mr. Barnes looks to his wife and then at Olivia and then back to me.

"And where is this knowledge of fashion coming from?" he asks.

"It's just a hobby. Something I fell into in high school."

"Hmm," Mr. Barnes says. He stretches a bit to talk to the gentleman sitting on the opposite side of his wife. Then he turns back to me.

"Sydney, this is my assistant Alex," he says, gesturing to the man he'd just been talking with. "He's going to take your information. I want to set up a breakfast meeting with you to talk more about this …hobby."

Breakfast? With Mr. Barnes? To talk? About fashion? About me?

"Uh, okay, yeah, okay." Alex walks up to me with an iPad and takes down my number.

"I'll call you tomorrow morning with the date, time, and place."

"Okay, sounds great. Thank you. And thank *you*, Mr. Barnes." I look at everyone around the table as I wave.

Olivia doesn't even bother to make eye contact as she finishes the last of her champagne.

Corey smiles and waves at everyone as he puts my arm through his.

"What was that?" I ask.

"What was what?" he responds.

When we get to our table, he pulls out my chair and makes sure that I'm under the table. He pushes too hard, and I slam into the table, knocking over my water glass towards Nicholas' plate.

"Oh, snap," Corey says.

I quickly grab as many napkins as I can, but Nicholas is already three feet away from his seat.

"Well, what is this? Are you trying to wash my dishes?" Nicholas says with both hands in his pockets. He looks at me with an amused smile.

"I'm sorry," I say through clenched teeth.

What a drop—to go from the highlight of my evening to the most embarrassing moment.

"See, that's why they don't need all of these cups. Accidents waiting to happen," Corey says. He shakes his napkin out of the fancy origami it was folded into and tucks it into the top of his shirt over his bowtie.

"Are you serious right now?" I ask in amazement.

"What?" he says innocently.

I put my hand over my head and wish the rest of this night away. With impeccable timing, the server comes over with the first course so I can eat my feelings. The second course immediately follows, and I feel my confidence coming back little by little. With each taste of the butternut squash soup, I close my eyes and drift away to a happier place, which, for now, is the bread that accompanies the soup. I shoot a glance at Nicholas and watch as he laughs with the gentleman next to him. *He sure does have a nice smile.*

"How many plates are we going to get at this thing?" Corey whispers.

"I don't know, but I'm going to enjoy every last one." Our entrée course comes after the soup, and then we are given dessert. The band is playing all the while, and I smile as I close my eyes to a bite of chocolate cake. *Merry Christmas to me.* A tap on my left shoulder knocks me out of my sugar enchantment.

"You still owe me a dance, you know." Nicholas winks, smiles, and then extends his hand. Before I can answer, someone taps on my right shoulder.

"You ready to head out?" Corey says as he stands up. I see him look at Nicholas and then look at me—two gentlemen standing between a seated lady.

"You want to leave now?"

"Yeah, I was—"

"Mr. Gutierrez, you weren't about to leave before you had a dance with me, were you?" Olivia takes Corey's hand and smiles while she sways to the dance floor.

My eyes narrow at the two of them, and the sickly feeling I felt at Luke + Barnes creeps back up. Why do I even have this feeling in the first place? I chug the rest of the water in my glass and stand up to take

Nicholas' hand, staring at Corey and Olivia the entire time.

Corey knew I was looking at them because he was looking right at me. This time he gives me the "what are you doing" look, but I turn around and face Nicholas.

He grabs my hand and puts his other hand on my waist as we twirl around on the dance floor. I keep swallowing my spit as my mouth becomes drier and drier the more turns we take.

The more we dance, the more my thoughts drift off in replaying the conversation I had with Mr. Barnes. I, Sydney Jamillah Humphries, just talked with the man leading the resurgence of the Renaissance man in America. I'm dancing with one of the most handsome men I've ever met in my life, and I just tasted the creamiest chocolate cake I ever had. I never want this snow-globe moment to end.

The music transitions to a much faster song, and I glance at Corey who's giving a head nod to Olivia and going back to the table. Nicholas and I continue dancing as I keep trying to look at what's going on back at the table.

"Everything okay?" Nicholas asks.

"Oh, yeah," I say with a smile and take another glance at the table.

"She's all bark and no bite, ya know."

"Right, just like a Pitbull."

He chuckles as he twirls me a few times and then dips me.

As I come back up, Corey is standing there with his hands in his pocket.

"Ready to go?" he asks.

I drop out of our ballroom stance. My teeth clench as I look to the floor in embarrassment. The night has yet to formally end, but here is Corey bussing up my dance with the most handsome guy I've ever met.

Could I just have five minutes?

"We're not finished with our dance," Nicholas says in a serious tone.

My head leans to the side to non-verbally communicate that I'm with Nicholas on this one.

"Sydney, we should go," Corey says.

"And I said we're not finished our dance," Nicholas says as he grabs my hand and puts it on his shoulder.

"No, it's okay Nicholas," I say as I remove my hand. *I'm going to regret this for the rest of my life, aren't I?* I tighten my lips as I walk over to my seat to grab my clutch.

Corey has more than enough money to actually *live* the life he sees here at the gala, yet he's constantly at Carina and I's apartment. I barely have space to breathe already and then—him. I sneak a quick glance at him and think back to when we were at Luke and Barnes buying his suit. He does look pretty handsome. *Ugh! What am I doing? Get it together, Sydney!*

"I would love to call you sometime," Nicholas says as he comes to his seat.

"Really?" I ask. Oh, wait, that was supposed to be an inside thought.

"Yeah," he says as he chuckles.

"Okay," I say, smiling. I continue to walk out of the ballroom, determined to not look Corey in the face. We walk to the foyer as the valet retrieves our vehicle. Looking at everywhere else but in Corey's face, I replay the night's events in my head again.

The blue, Ford pick-up pulls up, and Corey offers his arm for me to walk down the steps.

I swiftly decline as I pull my dress up to walk down the steps. I get into the car and stare out of the window like a kid on a long road trip.

"How come you haven't said anything?"

"What do you want me to say, Corey?" I ask slowly as I try to disguise my anger.

"*Something*. Anything."

"Well, thanks for bringing me tonight, and thanks for ending my dance early, and thanks for embarrassing me." I turn to the window in hopes of retreating to the mental snow globe I've created.

He lets out a sigh. "I was getting tired of being there. The fakeness, I could smell it from a mile away."

"Oh, is that why you danced with Olivia?"

"What, are you jealous?"

That response took me by surprise.

"No, I'm not jealous. Why would I be jealous?" *Am I jealous?* "You were *obviously* jealous that I was with Nicholas."

"I was *not* jealous. I just don't like him."

"You don't even know him."

"*You* don't even know him," he responds.

I cross my arms as I let out a sigh. "You weren't having fun, so you figured I shouldn't either."

"Sydney, I'm not leaving you there by yourself."

I'm angry, so why am I still feeling the flutters when he says my first name?

Not only am I annoyed with Corey, but now I'm annoyed at myself. We spend the rest of the drive in silence, which is fine with me. I go into the apartment and leave the door open for Corey.

Carina is in the kitchen washing dishes. "So?" she says with excitement, "How was it? Are you cooking for a week or is he wearing suits?"

I shake my head as I head straight to my room. I throw my clutch on my desk and flop to my bed. I can still salvage this night.

"No, no, no!" I yell to no one. I realize that I never gave Nicholas my phone number. I grab my pillow and scream all of my frustration into it. What else could wrong? I flip on my laptop and change into my pajamas as it warms up. I head to my *Wishlist* and begin adding things to my "Dream Apartment" board.

Yep, I'm going to make good on the promise I made to myself. I'm going to come out on top.

CHAPTER FIVE

DECEMBER 14TH

It's the day after the meeting with Mr. Barnes, and my hands are shaking as I turn on the espresso machine at the café. I listen to the sound of the rain and stare at all of the empty seats. Only a few weeks ago, I was sitting at that high-top by the window, and now I'm behind the counter. I wipe down the counters and all of the tables.

My meeting with Mr. Barnes couldn't have gone any better, at least I think so. I hope he thinks so too. We did, indeed, have the meeting at a new, exclusive restaurant that opened in the middle of the Center City on the top of a skyscraper. The restaurant had floor-to-ceiling windows that made me feel like I could touch the top of the Comcast building. How interesting it was to see the Philadelphia skyline from high up instead of down on the ground.

I wore my best outfit, besides my Christmas gala gown: a pair of cigarette pants, with classic black pumps, and a white, fitted turtleneck. I was giving a little Audrey Hepburn mixed with a dash of city-slicker with the black blazer I wore on top of the turtleneck.

Waiters brought a variety of pastries to our table, along with an assortment of fresh-squeezed fruit juices poured into white wine glasses.

Mr. Barnes asked me a bit about my upbringing and where I went to school. I mentioned to him a bit about Corey, Carina, and my grandmother.

"Ms. Humphries, I am quite impressed. Hmm, I have an idea. Look out for a call from me tomorrow."

And that was how the meeting ended. He had to run to another meeting but allowed me to stay and get whatever I wanted on his tab. Ever since I left the restaurant, I've been thinking of the million and one possibilities of what his idea could be and how I fit in to it.

I finish wiping everything down in the café, turn on the music, and unlock the door. The first hour is pretty slow. I can't be left with these thoughts in my head, so I do a duet with Ella Fitzgerald as she sings "Summertime."

"Ahem."

I'm pulled out of my concert by a customer who's entered the café.

Olivia.

"Good morning, Olivia."

She stands on the rain mat that I put out for customers to wipe their shoes. Passing the umbrella bin, she shakes the rainwater from her umbrella onto the floor.

"I'm sorry; do I know you?"

I purse my lips and clear my throat. "Sydney. From the Christmas gala. Corey's friend?"

"Oh, right. I always thought Cinderella was an interesting name. Caramel macchiato with double espresso."

She hands me cash, and I turn around to begin her order. We were on an even playing field at the gala. Here, it's back to reality. The machine whirls and whistles, and within minutes, her drink is complete.

"See you—"

But before I could even get the words out, she's out of the café and on to the rest of her life. The rest of her elaborate, travel-filled, stress-free life.

* * *

I blame Olivia for how the rest of the day went. I had to work a double because Tina called in sick. I put up with screaming babies who thought coffee looked better on the floor than in a cup. Some of them thought their juice looked better on me than in their sippy-cup.

And I saw more and more women and men in slick, fancy coats with beautiful bags and gorgeous wallets and money to burn. My eyes hurt from all the gigantic engagement rings I saw.

As I run to catch a bus to an emergency meeting for the church's Easter play, an impatient driver whips in front of the bus, spraying me with water and whatever else the city concocted for the day. I regret not taking the time to button up my coat before I left. I take a seat in front and close my eyes to will away—everything.

My phone keeps buzzing, but I don't answer. I close my eyes and soak in these few minutes I have to myself. What seems like only seconds were indeed minutes as I'm jolted awake by the bus driver slamming on his brakes. I look out the window and see my stop is next. I step off the bus and walk two blocks and then take a big breath in and out as I reach the double doors of the church.

"Sydney, you're late. I kept calling you. Eww, what happened to you?" Carina says as I take a seat next to her.

"I don't want to talk about it."

Christopher, head of the drama team, was saying something up front, but I zoned out. I dreamed of Chinese takeout, my pajamas, and a season of Dorian

Gray. I can't tell you when I started liking shows based in Nineteenth-Century England, but this is one of the best TV shows I've watched in a long time.

"So, you'll do it, Sydney?"

"Huh?"

Carina elbows me, and I look around.

"What? Who said my name?"

"Chris. He's asking about costumes for the play."

"What about costumes?"

"You think you could make some for us, Sydney?" Chris says. "I heard you were good with a needle and thread."

"Uh, I don't know. How many costumes do you need?" I ask Chris.

"Twenty?"

"Twenty?"

"Oh, c'mon, Sydney. We could really use your help. Besides, you have like three months before we start dress rehearsals." Carina says as she puts her arm around me.

What am I supposed to do? I can barely keep up with my own life with my job, let alone take on making costumes for twenty people. But if I don't do it, what will they think about me? How will they get their costumes?

"Okay, I'll do it."

Carina hugs me and pats me on the back. "This is going to be so much fun, I promise."

Yeah, fun for who?

The rest of the meeting goes by in a blur as my mind tries to compute how I'm going to produce twenty costumes by Easter. We get home, and I plop down in Corey's recliner.

"Hey, you have your own sofa," he says as he closes the front door to the apartment.

"Hey, you have your own house," I say.

Yep, it's time for that Chinese take-out.

I shower, change, and dig through the drawer full of take-out menus in the kitchen.

"Anybody want anything? I'm ordering Chinese," I say.

"Uh-oh. What's wrong?" Carina asks.

"What do you mean 'what's wrong?' Nothing's wrong. I'm perfectly fine."

"Chinese takeout is your version of retail therapy. What's wrong?"

"I promise I'm fine. Do you guys want anything?"

"I'm good," Corey says.

Carina points to her bowl of cereal as she takes a seat at the dining table.

She's not fine," Carina says to Corey. "She's gonna tell us soon enough. Just give her a minute," she says.

"So, how did that meeting go with Barnes?" Corey asks

"Ah, that was today," Carina says.

"Yeah, it was today. And that's Mr. Barnes to you, Corey," I say, "and it went really well. We were at this amazing restaurant with amazing views."

"What did he want to talk about?" Carina asks and puts a spoonful of cereal in her mouth.

"He said that he had an idea for something. Other than that, I don't know. He did say he'd call me today. He hasn't called yet.."

I find the menu and place my order. I can hardly wait for the food and need something to appease my growling stomach in the meantime, so I find some yogurt in the fridge. I plop down next to Carina at the dining table and put my head on her shoulders. She puts her head on top of mine, and we just sit there: her eating her cereal and me eating my yogurt. She really is like a sister to me. She knows that sometimes all I need is a moment to simply sit.

"What if you get a job?" Carina asks.

"Yeah, right, Carina," I say in disbelief. "There's no way Mr. Barnes would offer someone like me a job."

"Think about it, Humphries. Now you'd get to see Nicholas every Christmas," Corey teases.

Carina gasps. "Who's Nicholas?"

"He's someone I met at the Christmas gala."

She gasps again. "You met a guy ... and you didn't tell me?"

"Carina, it wasn't anything serious. I haven't talked

to him since the gala." I walk over to the sofa and grab a pillow. "And Corey didn't have to say anything." I hit him a few times, hoping to get my point across.

Nicholas—another fantasy, much like a job at Luke + Barnes—was something I wanted to keep close to me . . . a place where I could go if I needed a short, mental escape.

"Carina, you should've seen this dude. I had to check him a few times," Corey says.

"Check him?" I respond. "Hardly. Carina, he barely said two words to me. And there was nothing for Corey to check except for *you* checking out Olivia." I hit him a few more times with the pillow.

"Alright, you know what?" He grabs a pillow and a fight commences.

"Hold on, you two. Get to your corners," Carina says as she steps in between us.

Corey and I look at each other, and we know exactly what's going to happen next. Both of us hit her with our pillows, and she stumbles down onto the ground.

"Oh, you guys are going to get it!" Carina runs to the sofa to grab the last pillow as we all take shots at each other.

We can't really run around because the living room is too small, but we still had space to dodge attacks when necessary. Corey, Carina, and I all end up on the floor laughing into the pillow cushions. Our hair is all over the place, and our faces are red.

Corey gets a couple more hits off of Carina, but she calls a hard stop as she walks toward her room.

"Syd, your phone is ringing."

My food!

I answer the phone and quickly grab shoes to meet the delivery guy outside. Coming back up the elevator, I look at my phone and notice three missed calls and a voicemail from a number that's not saved in my phone. Unpacking the food on the dining table, I listen to the voicemail:

> "Hello, Sydney. This is Derek Barnes from Luke and Barnes. You seem to be a hard lady to reach this evening. I want to offer you a position as associate stylist at my Rittenhouse store. I was very impressed with your background and appreciate the passion that you have for the mission and vision of the brand. You're a quick problem-solver and are one for innovative and creative solutions. You can call this number when you receive this. I'll have Alex email you the paperwork to get you going. I hope to talk with you soon. Have a good evening."

The phone slips out of my hand onto the table.

My entire body locks up as tears begin to form in my eyes.

"Sydney, is everything okay? What happened?" Carina rushes to my side and puts an arm around my shoulder. "Eww, there's spit on the table."

I guess my mouth stayed open for a long time. Carina rocks me a little bit, and I look at my phone and then at her.

"Mr. ... Mr. Barnes ... Derek Barnes ... he offered ... he just gave me a ... a job."

Carina screams as she jumps up and down. "I knew it! I knew it! I told you he was going to give you a job." She hugs me so hard I almost fall out of the chair.

"This calls for a celebration! Emergency choco-spiced cookies coming right up!" Carina runs straight to the freezer to take out her cookie dough. She has a recipe for chocolate chip cookies where she adds a hint of cayenne and is by far the best cookie I've ever tasted in my life.

"Aw shoot, I think we're out of milk though. Corey! Can you run to the store to get milk? Carina asks.

Corey says nothing as he turns off the TV, puts on his shoes, and walks out the door.

I listen to the voicemail again, and again, and again. I've never heard anyone tell me something like this. Me? Innovative? A problem-solver? Creative?

Wait, what am I going to wear? I've already worn my best outfit.

I'll think about what to wear later. Right now, we celebrate because I, Sydney Jamillah Humphries, am a member of the Luke + Barnes fashion house. I close my eyes and take in the smell of the choco-spiced cookies.

Now, it's my time to shine.

CHAPTER SIX

JANUARY 10TH

It's my first day as an associate stylist at Luke + Barnes. I could afford to buy two new outfits I'll rotate out with different shirts and pants that I already own until I get my first paycheck. And boy, would that paycheck be a bump up from what I was making at the café. I could afford to buy these two outfits with one hour of pay because of how much I'll be making at the store—showroom. For good measure, I decide to stop by the café on my way in to get a congratulatory/good luck caramel macchiato.

"This one's on the house," Tina says as she's making my drink.

"We really miss you here," she says with a frown.

"It's only been a couple of days.

"We just hired this kid straight outta high school and he's already broken the espresso machine.

I put my hand over my mouth in shock.

"Thank you, Tina. You know this is going to be my regular coffee spot," I say as I walk backward to leave.

"It better!" she says as she waves.

Walking to the Luke + Barnes store seems different today. I stop in front of the double doors and take in a deep breath. Closing my eyes, I feel present in the moment. This new moment, the moment that will change my life forever.

"Excuse me," Olivia says from behind me as she opens the door and walks in and lets the door close behind her.

What else could I do but move to the side? I push my purse on my shoulder to try to catch the door before it closes.

"Here, let me help you."

I turn to see Mr. Platinum has held the door open for me.

"Thanks Mr. Plat—I mean Tristan."

"Do we know each other? Can I help you with something?"

"Yeah, um, today is my first day. I'm Sydney. Sydney Humphries."

"Sydney Humphries . . . Oh, yes, I remember you from the Christmas gala. You made quite an impression on Mr. Barnes. Well, let me formally introduce myself as your co-worker; I'm Tristan Barnes. No relation." He smiles as he offers me his hand.

I shake his hand. "It's nice to meet you again, Tristan. Where do I go?"

"You can follow me. We'll get you set up upstairs." He smiles as he scans a card next to the button for the fourth floor that he then presses.

"So, do you live in the city?" he asks.

"I do. I'm originally form Philly. Born and raised," I say.

When we reach the fourth floor, the doors open to a white-marble floor with a set of glass doors straight ahead that has Luke + Barnes Styling etched in white.

We walk a few feet to the doors, and he scans his card again, and we step onto hardwood floors inside the office. Directly out of a window straight ahead gives a delightful peek at the city skyline. These windows are laid into beautiful red brick that spans the entire length of the space. Five desks are spaced evenly in the room. Each desk has a glass tabletop with a huge Mac desktop computer, a small dock where an iPhone can be charged, and a tall, black, leather rolling chair to sit in.

Olivia is going back and forth between tapping her phone and typing on her keyboard.

"Tristan," she says without looking up from her screen.

"Olivia."

"And who's this?"

"Olivia, you saw her at the gala. She came here to get her dress for the gala. You didn't see her when you walked in?"

"I'm Olivia. I would shake your hand, but I'm busy."

My lips tighten. *Will she ever acknowledge me?* I notice the red on the bottom of her boots. Those are the same Christian Louboutin boots that I have on my *Wishlist*. Is there anything this woman doesn't have? Well, it doesn't matter. Soon enough, I'll be in her spot.

"I'm Sydney."

She continues typing at her keyboard, never breaking her gaze at her monitor to look at me.

Today is going to be a long day.

"Your desk is the third one in the middle, next to mine," Tristan says. "Grab that pad and pen there on your desk, and let's head to the conference room. We have a meeting."

I grab a pen, pad, and my coffee and follow Tristan to the conference room when I feel a pull on my wrist.

"Look, I get it," Olivia says. "You're a wide-eyed, bushy-tailed, young professional who finally got her break. But trust me, I've had four people quit who were in your position because they couldn't keep up. So, excuse me if I'm not so cordial. Let's see how long you last." She walks ahead of me, and I take a look around the room.

I can hear the *Hamilton* song, "My Shot," playing in my head, and I squint my eyes toward the conference room.

I am not throwing away my shot.

* * *

After the introductory meeting to the company, Tristan takes me around the showroom and goes over the way a stylist communicates with their clients. He calls it "LB Etiquette."

"And now you have the chance to try out that LB etiquette." His head leans in the direction of a guy who just walked into the showroom looking like he just stepped out of a GQ magazine. I brush imaginary lint from my pants as I walk toward him.

"Hi, my name is Sydney. Are you here for an appointment?" I smile as I put my hands behind my back. I sneak a glance at Tristan who mouths the word "handshake" as he opens his hand and motions towards Mr. GQ. I hurriedly look back at the gentleman and stick my hand out for a handshake.

Mr. GQ returns the handshake as he says, "I don't have an appointment. I didn't realize I needed one." A smirk forms on the side of his mouth that triggers heat to flush to my cheeks. His velvety voice caught me off guard.

"Oh, okay, that's no problem. Could I interest you in some water or coffee as you look around?"

We're still holding our hands in the handshake as I realize how much I have to stretch my neck to make eye contact. *I can't get flustered. Not now!*

"No, thank you. No water." Mr. GQ puts both hands in his pockets as he looks at me and then looks at Tristan.

I look at Tristan who quickly looks away and starts fiddling with a suit on a mannequin.

What do I say next?

"What brings you in today?"

"I want to buy a suit" he says matter-of-factly.

"What will the suit be for?"

Mr. GQ looks at Tristan and then at me. "A polo match."

"A polo match?"

"As a thank you from a client who gave me tickets to a polo game on Memorial Day. So, I'll need something breathable because it's going to be extremely hot. No color, I only wear black and gray. I heard you have some new ties, and I want to look at your cuff links."

"Alright, alright, take it easy on her." Tristan walks over with both hands in his pockets and then shakes Mr. GQ's hand.

"Sydney, this is my best friend, Darius. Darius, this is Sydney. Today is her first day."

"Nice to meet you, Sydney."

Why does everyone who has some kind of connection to Luke + Barnes look like a model?

I've never seen perfect teeth like Darius's. His smile beams a warmth that I wouldn't expect from a fashionably stiff guy like him. Although, I must say the shade of gray he's wearing compliments his brown skin perfectly. He has thick, curly hair sitting on top of his head that makes me think he's just starting to grow his hair out. *He would actually look nice in navy and white.*

The elevator door opens, and out walks Olivia. "Cindy. Tristan." She struts towards Mr. GQ and does a flirty wave. "Nice to see you again, Darius." She smiles and gets on her tip-toes to hug him.

"It's nice to see you too, Olivia. You look good."

"Thank you," she says as she flips her hair, and walks out of the showroom. Darius's eyes never left her as she walked out.

Man, I never have guys look at me like that.

"When are you going to ask her out?" Tristan asks to Darius.

"I'm taking my time, man. I'm taking my time."

"Sydney, we were just about to go to lunch. Did you want to come with us?" Tristan asks.

"Um, I don't know."

I then realized I never packed anything before

leaving this morning, and I'm trying to pace myself with spending until I get my first paycheck.

"C'mon, Sydney, it's Tristan's turn to pay," Darius says.

"Alright, then. Just let me get my things."

As I look down at my basic black slacks and teal turtleneck, an image of Olivia's outfit flashes through my mind. I quickly shake my head as if the image will just fall like a snowflake or a leaf…out of my head and onto the ground. Once I grab my things, the image is immediately replaced with a thought: what exactly do rich people talk about?

* * *

Here? Of all places, here?

Darius holds the door open for me as we walk into Parc, the French restaurant of my dreams.

We're greeted by the hostess who smiles and says, "Hello, Mr. Barnes. Shall I get your usual table?"

"Hello, Letitia. Yep, the usual."

Letitia grabs three menus and leads us to a table by the window toward the middle of the restaurant. We're seated and handed our menus. A server provides us with glasses of water and a basket of bread. I can smell the butter as the steam is still rising from the fresh-baked pieces of a baguette. The menu is printed in red ink on thick, cream, weathered paper, that gives it an Old-World feel. French jazz is playing softly in the background of many conversations and clanking silverware against white plates.

"So, what's your story, Sydney?" Darius asks. "How did you end up at Luke + Barnes?"

I replay the story of how I got to go to the Christmas gala, and Sophia, and Mr. Barnes.

"I bonded with Mr. Barnes' granddaughter which gave me an opportunity to talk with Mr. Barnes. I offered some suggestions, we had a meeting, and here I am." I take a sip of water.

"One word of advice, Sydney?" Tristan says, looking at me with earnest. "Don't let Olivia get to you. She's all bark and no bite. Trust me."

Nicholas said the same thing at the Christmas gala.

I dip a slice of bread into olive oil. "I don't know. She seems to have a very convincing bark if you ask me."

"Trust me, she knows you're good. That's why she's coming after you so hard. She was always the star employee, but with Mr. Barnes bringing you in, she now has competition."

"Olivia said that there were four other people in my position who quit because they couldn't take it."

"No, they couldn't take *her*. As evil as she may seem, she's still one of the best stylists in the city."

"Well, I do have my degree in marketing as well," I say with a sense of pride, "so, I can assist with campaigns, email blasts, styling for photo shoots, and stuff." All the confidence that I had ten seconds ago left like a quickly deflated balloon. I stare at the table.

"Hey, don't shrink back now. Mr. Barnes hired you for a reason. You deserve to be here just as much as Olivia. And there's one thing you have that Olivia doesn't—me. I got your back."

I force a smile and stare into my water glass. What have I got myself into?

CHAPTER SEVEN

MARCH 7TH

Corey, Carina, and I slide into a booth at Jones.

"Sydney would pick the cool, fancy place in Center City," Carina says as she looks up at the exposed pipes and duct work crawling along the ceiling, painted gray and pendant lights sprinkling between them. The color palate of gray and black with a pastel orange and green gives me modern California vibes with a nod to classic Palm Beach.

It's been quite a while since I've seen my friends. If it's not work, I'm at the apartment sleep from exhaustion. Tristan has been getting me away from my desk more and more as I accompany him to at-home styling appointments—only for elite clientele—and working the floor of the showroom. I've been to a few cocktail parties here and there, introducing myself to society as the newest Luke and Barnes employee. I guess you can call it my professional debutante ball.

"This place isn't fancy," I say.

We place our orders, Carina heads to the restroom, and Corey looks at me for an uncomfortable amount of time.

"Why are you looking at me like that?"

He looks down at his glass and then back at me. "You like your job?"

"How nice of you to actually care—"

"Don't do this—"

"Don't do what?" I ask incredulously. This is something that I've been noticing since I began my new job. I didn't think I would talk to him about it here, but, no time like the present, right?

"You haven't mentioned anything about my job since I've started. You haven't said a 'congratulations' or 'I'm happy for you, Sydney'... nothing."

"So, you actually like working there?"

"Why wouldn't I? Corey, I'm literally living out my dream. Granted, this dream comes with little-to-no social life, but I guess my work friends are my new social life. You have to meet Tristan and Darius. They are really cool. It's almost like I'm their little sister or something which is odd to say because they are so handsome—"

"More handsome than Nicholas?" Corey asks as he bats his eyes playfully.

"Whatever. I don't think I'll ever see him again. But *your* girlfriend Olivia is winning gold medals in the looks department every time she comes to work."

Corey moves his finger around on the table as if he's drawing something. I wonder if he still thinks about her. *I wonder if he thinks about me.*

"For the past two months, I've been shadowing Tristan and doing paperwork. I've tried to shadow Olivia a few times, but I personally think she sabotaged the entire day to make it look like I was incompetent."

"Really?" he asks.

"Yeah. In fact, why don't you ask her. I'm sure you guys have a date planned or something, right?"

Corey balls up the paper napkin that was under his drink and throws it at me. He sits back against the booth and stirs his water. I lean back, cross my arms, and let my head fall back on the booth.

Carina comes back from the bathroom, looks at both of us, and sits down slowly.

"What happened while I went to the bathroom?"

"Nothing," We both say in unison.

"Now that's a lie." She sips her water and fiddles with the saltshaker.

I take a deep breath. "Corey thinks I shouldn't be working at Luke and Barnes."

"I never said that."

"You never said *anything*."

"I just think you need to be careful is all. It was bad enough you were run ragged by your job at the café."

"I wasn't run ragged. I liked that job."

"Syd, we barely saw you."

"I showed up to church when I was supposed to, and I hung out with you guys whenever I could. Now with this job, I'm doing the costumes for the Easter play…"

The costumes. I haven't even started the costumes.

"You can show up all you want, but your heart isn't in it. Your heart hasn't been in it," Corey says as his voice gets a bit louder.

My heart rate goes up. *He doesn't know me.*

"What are you saying—"

"You know what I'm saying," he interrupts, "You've just been going through the motions. You think no one knows, but *I* know. You forget that I *know* you, Sydney."

I hate that he knows. I hate that he can tell when I'm sad and when I'm angry, even when I say that I'm fine. He's always been able to see right through me.

"Why are you being a jerk about this?" Carina elbows Corey in the arm.

"*I'm* the one being a jerk? Sydney's being fake, and *I'm* the jerk?" he asks in shock.

"Oh, so I'm fake now?"

He was right, but it's only a figment of my imagination until someone says it out loud. And I'm not going to allow him to continue to say it out loud.

"I know you didn't make it—"

"Carina, don't even go there," Corey says, frowning. "This has nothing to do with the playoffs."

"Then why are you so bitter about Sydney's job?"

"I'm not bitter."

"Then what is it?"

"I just don't want her to leave!" he shouts.

Everyone's head turn in our direction.

I let myself fall against the back of the booth.

Carina fiddles with her napkin.

Corey looks down at the table.

"Look," he says then sighs. "I'll always support you; I just want you to promise me that this won't be a repeat of high school."

I clench my teeth and close my eyes as I try to shove away the memories. Each year had a different story to tell, all ending in a fight, all ending in hurt. Being called "patches" was the least of it. The table is quiet as I take a few deep breaths.

"This is my chance to make something of myself," I say. "To distance myself as far away from high school as I possibly can. It's four years too late, but it's finally happening." I would love to see the faces of the people now when I tell them that I'm an Associate Stylist at

Luke + Barnes. I bet they never thought this could happen to *this* orphan girl.

"Just make sure you don't distance yourself from us in the process," he says with a sideways smile.

"I promise."

Carina dabs the corner of her eyes with a napkin.

"Please tell me you're not crying," Corey says as he sips his ginger ale.

"I'm not crying. My eyes are sweating."

I burst out into laughter.

"Cindy?"

I recoil at the sound of the familiar voice. "Olivia?"

"Hello, Corey," she says. It's nice to see you again."

"So, *this* is Olivia," Carina says quietly as she brings her lemonade to her lips.

Olivia is back in the trenches, literally, as she's wearing a black trench coat with yellow heels. Her hair is in a high ponytail, and her red lipstick pops against her tanned skin.

"And you are?"

"Carina. I am Carina, Corey's sister." Carina could move a bus with all of the intensity in her eyes as she looks at Olivia.

"Olivia, did you want something?" I ask.

"Yes, you. You're not answering your phone."

"I'm off."

"You're never *off*. You might have breaks, but you're never off."

"How did you know I'd be here?"

" I didn't. I saw you through the window and suggested we stop in and say hi."

Tristan comes beside Olivia and smiles.

Carina instantly tenses up and kicks me under the table. She uses her widened eyes to point in the direction of Tristan. I've rarely seen Carina get flustered by handsome men, but I guess Tristan is the exception this time.

"We need to do more than say hi. You should be coming to this party with us."

"She doesn't have to, Olivia. Let her live," Tristan says.

"If she wants to be a part of this business then she needs to know it's not what you know but *who* you know, and she won't learn that if she doesn't meet people."

"I can't go to a party looking like this." My jeans and turtleneck sweater are not appropriate for any function Olivia is attending. "My apartment is all the way on the other side of the city."

Olivia looks like she gives up on me. Like I'm a disappointment.

"C'mon Tristan," she sighs as Tristan allows her to walk in front of him.

"Don't let this get to you. We'll talk on Monday," Tristan whispers to me right before he leaves.

"Guys, I think I should go," I say as I get up.

"What? Are you serious? We already put our food order in," Carina says.

— 88 —

"And so it begins," Corey says as he leans back against the booth.

"Stop it. Nothing is *beginning*. Olivia's right, I gotta get to know people in the business if I'm going to make something of myself—"

"And that's the most important thing, right?" Corey says mockingly as he rolls his eyes. "You know what? Just go."

"Corey, I—"

"Go!" He shouts again and people are looking at us—again. He slams his napkin on the table. Carina can't even make eye contact with me.

Don't they know that sacrifices come with every job? Like the many times I've tasted Carina's meals, helped her type out her recipes, and helped her shoot most of her videos.

And Corey has absolutely no excuse because I've been to every last one of his football games since he was eight—never missing one. It's Sydney's time to shine, and now my friends are nowhere to be found. I tried to invite them to parties, but they don't want to come. They haven't even visited the store to come in and say hi or go to lunch like Darius does with Tristan. It gets exhausting being the friend who is expected to support everyone else but doesn't get the support back.

I need a break.

I'm going to this party.

CHAPTER EIGHT

MAY 28TH

Normally for Memorial Day, Corey, Carina, and I binge-watch as many Marvel movies as possible. It looks like this year I'll be breaking the tradition. Turns out that polo match Darius talked about when we first met is a real thing—like a *big* thing. Olivia told me it's the first major event of the summer social season. There's also such a thing as a summer social season.

It's crazy the life you live when you jump tax brackets. Because I'm an employee of Luke + Barnes—and a new one at that—I need to be at said polo game to represent the brand and schmooze with all the well-to-dos. I was only given a week's notice, but I found time during lunch and early in the morning to curate the best look to help me fit in with the crowd.

I realize I left my business cards at the office, so I take a quick detour to the showroom to get them. As soon as I close the double doors behind me, I hear knocking.

"Darius, what are you doing here?"

"I completely forgot about the polo game."

"Okay," I say confused.

"I need a suit. I've never been to a polo game before, but I think my three-piece situation might be too stuffy."

Do you ever not wear a suit?

"You need me to style you now? I have to go back home and get dressed and then catch a train so I can get there on time."

"I'll drive you. It's the least I can do. We can come fashionably late, if anything."

I bite on my lower lip and look around. *Think Sydney, think.* "Okay, I'll help you. But you can't fight me on choices, we don't have time for a full consultation."

"I trust you completely."

"Follow me."

Running around the showroom like someone hit the fast-forward button on a movie, I remember an ivory, linen suit. It's our newest arrival of summer suits. I motion to a mannequin toward the back of the showroom.

"Absolutely not." Darius scrunches up his face and shakes his head.

"Hey, you said you trust me completely."

"But that's not me."

"You don't know that. You've limited yourself to wearing black and gray because that's what your profession calls for. This won't be a stuffy lawyers convention; this is a summer game with the who's who of Philadelphia and the surrounding area in attendance. You want to make an impression and get more clients? You have to get out of the box. And this is out of the box." Finding the pieces on the rack near the mannequin, I hold the suit up. "Here, try it on."

As he tries on the suit, I run upstairs and grab my business cards. I come back down and see him standing on the circular platform in front of mirrors.

"Whoa." *Again, an inside thought outside.*

"What do you think?"

"Uh …"

The suit looked good on him. The ivory color compliments his caramel brown skin perfectly. *We'll need brown loafers … and a silver watch but no cuff links.* It seems like it's taking me thirty minutes to make it to the platform, but once I get there, I stand on the balls of my feet to unbutton the top two buttons of his shirt. I roll up his jacket sleeves and then his shirt sleeves. I cuff the bottom of his pants, and then run around to find the brown loafers. *Perfect*. Darius does a full turn with his arms out. He seems unsure of himself.

"Trust me, Darius. This is it. You need to wear more color!"

He laughs as he turns back around to face the mirror.

We leave his other suit in the store and plan to get it after the game. Getting into his black, Mercedes convertible, we arrive in front of my apartment in fifteen minutes.

Did I just ride in the Batmobile?

"Would you mind if I used your restroom?" he asks.

I don't want him to see how I live. It's bad enough he now knows *where* I live. There's a chance for a clean slate, a fresh image, and Darius is ruining it.

"Uh, sure. You can come up."

I nervously tap my foot on the floor of the elevator until we make it to the sixth floor. As soon as the doors open, I grab my keys from my pocket and open the door.

Running past Carina, I say, "Carina, this is Darius. He has to use the restroom. I have to get ready for the game."

"Wait, what?" she asks with a mouth full of chips. Her hair is in a messy bun, and she's wearing one of Corey's sweatshirts with a pair of basketball shorts.

"Darius, he needs to use the restroom. I have to get ready."

I rush into my room and leave them to themselves. I hate getting ready in a rush. It feels like something always gets left unchecked or slips through the cracks. My strapless, pastel-yellow dress is laying on my bed with a pair of white, chunky, heels. I'm feeling the vintage Palm Springs vibe again.

Carina comes into my room without knocking as I'm half dressed. "Girl, who is that?"

"Carina!"

She closes the door quickly.

"You bring a guy up in here, and I look like this?"

"What are you talking about? You look fine."

"Sydney—"

"Carina, I can't talk right now. I gotta go."

With some gel, I wet my hair and slick it down into a bun at the top of my neck. Makeup is minimal but effective with blush-pink eyeshadow and light-brown lipstick. I grab a pair of diamond earrings I bought as a congratulatory gift with my first paycheck and walk into the living room, leaving Carina still in my room.

Darius stands up from the sofa as Corey is walking in.

"Who are you?" Corey barks out.

I wish Carina never gave Corey a key.

"Corey, this is Darius. We were just leaving." I nudge Darius toward the door as he tries to shake Corey's hand.

"What do you mean *leaving*? You're not staying? Where are you going?" Corey puts grocery bags on top of the dining table. "Also, Chris called me, he's been trying to get in touch with you about the costumes. You haven't been answering your phone."

Dang! The costumes. I let my shoulders fall as I slowly open the door and let Darius leave first.

"I haven't even started on those costumes yet, and I have a work event to go to," I say, standing in the doorway.

"You haven't started on the costumes?" Carina asks as she comes to the dining table to unpack the groceries. "Sydney, the play is in a month, and we haven't been fitted. There's twenty people in this play."

"Look, okay, I'm sorry. I won't be able to do it!"

"You won't be able to do it, and you're just now telling us?" Corey comes from behind the table and into the living room.

I inhale a woodsy smell—cologne—and feel the warmth of someone behind me. I turn around to see Darius standing there, eyes locked on Corey. I forgot for a moment that he was with me.

"If my job needs me, then I'm going to do what I need for my job."

"And what about us?" Corey asks. "What about the church? What about us?"

Even with my anger continuing to rise, there's a tickle in my throat at the sound of him saying *us* twice. I breathe in slowly, but I can still feel my ears getting hot. I look at my watch, and at the rate at which we're going, Darius and I will be at least ten minutes late. I give up. What else am I to do? I never would've thought I'd have to choose between my dream and my friends, but if my friends won't come along for the ride then . . .

"Look, you guys will be able to figure it out. There are lots of costumes shops in the city. I'm sure you guys will be able to find something."

"We wouldn't have to if you would've made the costumes," Carina says

"You were so busy with your new life . . ." Corey walks closer and closer. Darius slightly nudges me to the side so he's standing slightly in front of me.

"Can I help you?" Corey says as he gets close to Darius.

I've never seen Corey fight, and I don't want to start now.

"Okay, well look, I'm sorry to disappoint you, okay?" I say getting back in front of Darius. "I'm sorry that all Sydney can contribute to this friendship is disappointment. I'm sorry that I'll never amount to anything at work and never amount to anything in my personal life so all I can do is just make promises I can't keep just to keep everybody happy. I guess we're *all* guilty of it now—promising to be there for each other, promising to have each other's backs, promising to never give up on each other. Well, I'm sick and tired of broken promises—on both ends. I'm done."

I slam the door and hear Darius come right behind me. My eyes cloud with tears making it hard to see the elevator. My face gets hot, and I keep swallowing my spit to stop the tears from coming all the way down. I refuse to ruin my makeup, and I refuse to ruin this day.

* * *

You can hear an ant walk with the amount of silence that fills the car on the ride to the polo match. I'm grateful Darius doesn't press me into talking about anything. The drive is scenic and gives me time to freshen up my makeup and sit with my thoughts. I don't want to replay everything that took place, but my mind has a habit of betraying my feelings.

I watch the trees go by in hopes that the memories would go by as quickly. If no one else will support me, if no one else cares about my dreams, if no one else cares about my happiness, I'll just make sure to care about myself. *Always wins in the end.* I'll make sure of it.

Sydney Jamillah Humphries will be the last woman standing.

CHAPTER NINE

MARCH 28ᵀᴴ
LATER THAT DAY

Once we arrive to the match, I breathe in the fresh air. Is it a court? A field? What is the correct term? I'll have to find out a lot of things about the sport before I put my foot in my mouth.

Darius offers me his arm, and I take it, allowing my dress to flow behind me in the wind. I'm wearing my sunglasses and hold my head high. No one else has to know about what happened. No one has to know that I'm sad. *Sydney Jamillah Humphries. SJH. SJH.* I repeat this over and over as we get closer to the crowd.

A huge Cape-Cod-styled house sits to the far left of an open grass field cut off by a small, white fence.

I can't tell if the game has already started or if they're just warming up.

"To be honest, I don't actually know where I'm going. I've never been to one of these things before," Darius says.

"It's okay. *They* don't have to know that. Let's go where we hear the crowd."

The seats in the observation part of the field are mostly empty, but I see people walking and sitting outside the house farther down.

I gently lead Darius inside the house where we find drinks flowing and people huddled in groups. I could go for a drink right now. A strong drink.

I swore off drinking, remember. Don't do it. It's not worth it.

The house is filled with lots of laughter, and servers are walking around with trays of the tiniest bites I've ever seen. *Looks like I'll need to make a stop later.* There's a grand, marble staircase to my right and seating to my left with a bar toward to the back.

"Hey, Darius!"

We both turn to see a couple men coming toward us.

"I thought you said this was your first time here," I say to him. I put more of my arm through his and place my right hand on his bicep. He touches my hand as he greets the two men.

"John, Tom. What are you guys doing here?"

Darius lets go of my arm as the two, older, fair-skinned men with matching toupees shake his hand.

"And who is this lovely lady with you?" asks the gentleman with coke-bottle glasses.

"Sydney." I say as I reach out my hand. "Sydney Humphries. It's nice to meet you."

One of the men shakes my hand then turns to Darius. "Oh, she's a keeper, Darius." The man gulps the last of his drink.

"Tom and John are two of the partners at my firm," Darius tells me.

"We'll be adding Darius to that list pretty soon. I have no doubts."

Darius smiles and briefly looks at the floor. "So, what brings you guys here?"

"Oh, our wives always come here to hear about the latest gossip. Gossip for them, free drinks for us!"

All three laugh, and I simply stand there in hopes that a server would come by with a tray of *something*.

"What brings you here, Darius?"

"My client, Fred Perkins, he gave me tickets as a thank you."

"Yes, I heard good things from Fred. I tell you, Ms. Sydney, Darius is one of the best lawyers we have in this city. In fact, I almost didn't recognize you without your three-piece-suit."

"You can give her all of the credit for that. She's Luke and Barnes' new head stylist."

What? Maybe he misspoke. Surely, he knows I'm not head over anything. I just started a few months ago.

"Any person who can get you to *not* wear a tie is A-plus in my book. You know, my anniversary is coming up, and I want to look spiffy for the misses," Tom says.

"Oh sure. Here's my card. Be sure to give me a call whenever you're ready." I smile and hand him my business card.

"And I'm speaking at a conference next month," John says.

I hand a business card to him as well. *We just got here, and I'm already giving away business cards.* Darius and the gentlemen do more laughing, and I catch the eye of a server and grab a bite—literally. A lot of the women are wearing light, flowy dresses with huge beach hats and sunglasses. I missed that memo completely.

I stand there and smile so that it looks like I'm engaged in the conversation. *I wonder what Olivia's wearing.* It seems like Olivia may be making a fashionably late entrance as well. I'm not able to locate her in the crowd.

I notice a lot of older people here but also people my age as well. I grab more bites and continue smiling while Darius says his goodbyes to the two gentlemen. As the gentleman walk away, a slight breeze brings a familiar, woodsy smell to my nose. I take in the scent and continue to follow Darius.

We make it toward the back of the house and see a cabana that has a band, lounge chairs, and a few people dancing. Getting closer, I see Olivia in a yellow dress similar to mine, laughing with Nicholas, touching him on his back and arms.

Like she really laughs. She doesn't care. Wait, Nicholas and I aren't together, so why do I care?

"Olivia, It's good to see you," I say. "How are you doing?" *Do I sound as phony as I feel?*

Olivia looks up as if Darius is ruining her moment.

"Darius—and well, nice of you to show up, huh? Hello, Simby."

SJH.

"Olivia, you know my name, and I'm sick of you treating me like you don't. I understand that you may not like me, but you *will* treat me with respect." Everyone else fades away as I lock my glare on her. "Mr. Barnes has made me a stylist, and I *know* I'm a good one. You're just going to have to get over it. Now, if you'll excuse me, I'm going to find some real food in this place."

Sweat creeps up on my temples, and I slow my pace. My heart is beating at a pace I didn't know it could get to. My stomach is making its way up as well. *Where is the restroom?* In search for a restroom, I suddenly feel a hand on my elbow.

"Sydney."

I turn around to see Nicholas standing there in a navy-blue suit with the arms and legs rolled up. His hair is in a bun on the top of his head. I take a big gulp of nothing and look for where the water is located.

"Hey," is all I could get out.

"What was that back there?" He points with his thumb back to the scene of the crime.

"Nicholas, you have no idea how much Olivia has been mean to me the entire time that I've been at Luke and Barnes."

"You're at Luke and Barnes now? Whoa, that's awesome. "

"It would be if Olivia wasn't as welcoming as a cactus."

"Look, Olivia can be a bit of an ice princess—"

"A bit'? That's an understatement."

"I've never seen anyone talk to her like that though. Ha! You've definitely made an impression; I can tell you that."

I shrug as I catch the eye of a server and ask them for water.

"So, who's that guy you're with?"

Looks like Mr. Spencer is suffering from a case of jealousy, huh?

"If you must know, he's a friend of Tristan's."

"You guys serious?"

"Is there something you want to ask me?"

"No, I mean I was just curious if you were seeing anybody?"

"Why are you curious?"

Nicholas shuffles back and forth with both hands in his pockets. A breeze from the outside takes a wisp of hair from behind his ear and blows it in his face. My heart continues its accelerated pace as I try not to assume that the most handsome man I've ever met in my life might ask me out on a date. I've never been on a date before.

Dates were non-existent for me in high school and in college. In high school, guys didn't want to touch me with a ten-foot pole; and in college, I was too into my studies to care what guys thought. I only wanted to get the best grades possible and hustle to get a job that I could throw in the faces of all those people who contributed to my horrible high-school experience. Interaction with handsome men of this caliber—or any caliber—is a new thing for me.

But I'm Sydney Jamillah Humphries, Associate Stylist at Luke + Barnes, so I need to remain cool and act as if I'm not new to this.

Nicholas continues to look at me as he smiles and rocks back and forth on his heels. "Have dinner with me."

Before I could get my answer out, a distinguished-looking woman comes alongside of Nicholas with a glass of champagne in her hand. She smelled faintly of flowers and wore a white, linen dress with gold earrings. Her gray hair was cut just below her ears, and her neck was laced with pearls.

"Are you Sydney Humphries?"

"Yes, yes I am." I say in the likes of Frasier Crane. *What is this new accent?*

"My husband made mention that you will be styling him for our anniversary. Do you style women as well?"

"Absolutely." I take out my card and tell her to set up a consultation. Another woman came up immediately after her in which I told her the same thing

After that, I had different women and men ask for my services throughout the party. Then I realize all of my business cards are gone, so I take the opportunity to go the restroom and get a second round of bites.

I take a peek out onto the field and look at a game that's well underway. I don't see Darius within a turn of my head, so I find a seat by myself out at the field. It feels like only five minutes go by before seats begin to fill up around me. Nicholas takes the seat directly next to me and rests his ankle on top of his other knee.

"So, you never answered my question," he says.

I turn to him and see him looking at the field.

"And what question was that, Mr. Spencer?"

"Oh, so I'm Mr. Spencer now, huh?" he says with a light chuckle. "Have dinner with me. Tonight."

"I have plans," I say, trying to keep from smiling.

He looks at me and it's almost as if he can read me like a book.

"I don't believe that for a second."

"And why is that?"

"You wouldn't have more work to do because *this* is your work event. From what I remember, you don't do much outside of work but go home or to church. So, I'm willing to bet that you were just going to go home and do nothing. Besides," he says, cocking his head sideways, " I know as much as you do that there's something between us and that you want to have dinner with me as much as I want to have dinner with you." He gives me a smile out of the corner of his mouth, and the breeze carries the deep, musky tones of his cologne right to my nose as if giving me my answer.

"Alright then, Mr. Spencer. I will have dinner with you tonight."

This time I make sure to give him my number and agree to have him pick me up at eight p.m.

I see the shadow of someone sit down next to me and turn to see that it's Mr. Barnes.

"Mr. Barnes! Hello, sir, how are you doing?"

"Sydney. I'm doing well." He nods to Nicholas. "Nicholas."

"Sir." Nicholas gets up and goes back into the house.

"You seem to be the buzz of today's match," Mr. Barnes says.

"I'm sorry?"

"Everyone's talking about you. Apparently, what you did with a gentleman named Darius spoke volumes."

"It was an accident how everything came about, really."

I begin to tell Mr. Barnes about how everything went down.

"You have truly surprised me, Sydney Humphries. Tristan tells me you're a joy to work with and that you've been learning quickly about the procedures and processes at the store. Clearly, you're good at what you do, and now that you're acclimated to the inner workings of Luke and Barnes, I think you're ready to be bumped up to Head Stylist."

What?

"What? For real? I mean, oh my goodness. Mr. Barnes. Thank you so much."

"Of course, it comes with a bump up in pay, but you'll also be going to the fashion shows in all of the major cities for the fall: New York, Paris, London, Milan …"

He says more, but my whole body goes numb. I, Sydney Jamillah Humphries, will be travelling outside of the United States to go to Fashion Week. In

Paris? And London? I can't move. Mr. Barnes's lips stop moving, so I take it he's stopped talking.

"Thank you so much. Truly, I'm so grateful for this opportunity."

He gets up, and I pull my phone out of my purse to call Carina.

Oh wait.

I put my phone back in my purse and get up to find Darius. As I walk back into the house, I overhear Olivia in mid-sentence.

"And she thinks she can just walk in here and take *my* trip to Paris? Oh, she has another thing coming."

Another thing coming? What does she mean by that? My ears begin to get hot. *No Sydney, this is supposed to be happy times. You're going to Fashion Week, and you have a date with Nicholas.*

I find Darius at the bar and tell him the good news.

"Syndey, that is awesome! We have to celebrate."

"I'm actually going to dinner with Nicholas tonight."

Darius's face falls a bit as he tries to maintain a smile. "Okay. Be careful."

"Be careful about what?"

"Just be careful is all. I'm happy for you. Did you tell Tristan?"

"No, I haven't seen him yet." I look around to see if Tristan is nearby, but he's nowhere to be found. I get a Coke from the bar and take an empty seat. Olivia's shell of a threat is still churning in my mind. Is she going to try to sabotage me going to Fashion Week? I still have about three months before my travels begin.

I stir my Coke and look around at all of the people who are laughing and drinking and dancing. That should be me, but I'm sitting here in a rut because some lady has it out for me.

I down the last of my Coke. *No, high school will not repeat itself.* Olivia may have something up her sleeve, but so do I.

So do I.

CHAPTER TEN

AUGUST 31ST

The first thing I did with my new raise is buy a new wardrobe: dresses, skirts, blouses, shirts, heels, watches . . . you name it. Olivia isn't the only one who can rock a nice bun with a pencil skirt. The polo game on Memorial Day changed my entire life. With Darius as my walking portfolio and technically my first client, my phone has been ringing off the hook for styling services. People call about anniversaries, work parties, holiday parties, and lots of other functions.

Tristan has become like a brother as he continues to encourage and support me in this new role.

Corey and Carina? Not so much. Avoiding the inevitable conversations that I can feel brewing is becoming easier as I'm invited to more dinner parties and outings. I don't have the bandwidth to deal with what I know they're going to say. Besides, I'm still riding the high of this promotion. Church has become non-existent at this point which is fine with me. It was holding me back anyway.

Nicholas took me to dinner at Butcher & Singer. He wanted to keep it a surprise, not knowing that I'd previously worked there—and he'll never know. I recognized a few people who tried to start conversations, but I kept it short and sweet.

"I used to come here a lot," I told him.

As the night went on, he wanted to learn more about my history and background, but I kept putting the conversation back into his court by making sure I answered as vaguely as possible. He doesn't need to know my life story. Besides, I'm a head stylist now; that's all that matters. My first date ended with a kiss that I'll be dreaming about while I'm at Fashion Week. I invited him to come with me, but he said he has a lot of work to do.

The time to pack for my trip to Europe has arrived. I need to take enough clothes for a month as I'm going from New York to London to Milan and then to Paris. Every time I say it, my cheeks hurt because I'm smiling so much. I'm in my room packing when I hear footsteps stop at my door.

"You going somewhere?" Carina asks in a disappointed tone.

"Yeah. I'll be in Europe for a month."

"Whoa, Europe? That's cool," she says, maintaining the same tone.

"Yeah."

She stands there as I continue to lay out clothes from every drawer and hanger from my closet.

"What's up?" I ask.

"I just don't like that we're not talking right now. You didn't even tell us you were going to Europe."

I put a few more items in my suitcase and sit on my bed. This is exactly what I was trying to avoid. I sigh and rub my pants as if I'm trying to get something off of them. I take a second to look at Carina and think about Corey.

"It seems like you guys haven't cared about my job since I've started, so why *would* I tell you?"

"Because we're your friends," she says as if it were a no-brainer.

But it's not.

"Are you?" I asked.

Her eyes get big and her arms drop to her side. "Are you serious right now? You're questioning our friendship?"

"I got pizza!" Corey yells as I hear the front door shut. "Hello! Anybody home?"

"We're in here," Carina says with her eyes still on me.

I put my head in my hands as I feel a headache coming on. They've been coming on more often as my schedule gets increasingly bigger. I reach for the pain meds I've been taking for the past few months. This is the last bit of stress I need. I close my eyes and envision myself at the front row of the Chanel fashion show, another dinner date with Nicholas, which I'm supposed to have before I leave—anything that will get me away from here.

I'd tried a glass of red wine when I was at Butcher & Singer, and it wasn't that bad. Granted, it's definitely an acquired taste, but I feel like I could use a glass or two of that right now.

Corey comes to the door standing behind Carina. "What's going on? Are you moving out?"

"She's going to Europe," Carina says while I say, "I'm going to Europe."

"Europe? By yourself? Why?" Corey asks. I can see concern in his eyes, but I wish I didn't have to see his face at all. My goal was to get away and tell them at the last minute so there wouldn't be room for things like this. I have to take in a concerned look on their faces, their crossed arms, and their spicy tones.

"Yes. I'll be fine. It's a work trip." I stand up from the bed and continue putting clothes into my suitcase.

I don't bother to fold them at this point. I think I'm going to spend the few nights I have left in a hotel before I leave.

"She just asked me are we even her friends which is why she didn't tell us about Europe," Carina says, looking at me.

"Oh, for real? That's how you feel?" Corey asks.

"C'mon y'all. I don't have time for the double team right now."

"You think because we're not supporting your foolishness that we're not your friends? It's—"

"Foolishness?" I interrupt Corey. "So, my job is foolishness? My dreams are foolishness?" I grab clothes and throw them into the suitcase.

"Oh, c'mon with this song and dance act about your dreams," Corey says.

"This isn't some song and dance act, Corey. This is my life. And up until this point you guys were involved in it. Maybe a little bit too much—"

Corey's eyes grow wide, and he gently moves past Carina and steps into my bedroom. "Sydney, how can you just throw away almost twenty years of friendship?"

"I should be asking you the same question. Who was it that was there for *every* football game and even helped you work on new plays? Whose shoulder did you cry on when you didn't get into your first choice of school for college? Who was there day and night when you tore your ACL and had to get surgery? *I* was.

"And Carina, I can just list off the many times I've stayed up late with you working on recipes and helping you shoot and edit your videos. But yet the moment Sydney has something going for herself, all of sudden it's foolishness." I throw more clothes into the suitcase as an exclamation point. I can't believe they're fighting me on this. They know that I'm right.

"It wouldn't be foolishness if you made time for the things that really matter," Carina says.

"Oh, so you guys are bitter because I can't make time for you? This is my job, Carina! Corey's away with football, and there's no uproar about that."

"Sydney, you know Corey's in the dang NFL; of course, he's going to travel."

"My point exactly! So, my job isn't legitimate enough for you? Are you mad because now *you* guys have to be the ones supporting and encouraging instead of me?"

"You know what? I quit. Have fun in Europe." Carina leaves.

Corey stands there looking at me. "You really don't get it, do you? It's *because* we care about you that we're telling you this. It's like you get around those people, and all of sudden you turn into this other person. Another person I really don't like. It's almost like it's high—"

"Shut up. Don't say it." I sit on the bed and put my hands in my head again. Corey's volume was soft, but his tone was firm. *How dare he bring that up again.* I can hear the taunts and feel the wads of paper being thrown at me again. Silence consumes the rest of what was our conversation. I can't do it anymore. I can't make the best friends I've ever had understand my heart without reliving those painful memories. I refuse to.

"You know what? Since you guys don't like this new Sydney that's emerging, I'll make it easier on you guys. I'll move out. I don't even know why I'm saying this to *you*; you don't even live here. Well, now you can save all the money you need to, Mr. Cheap-O, and live with your sister. All I wanted was a better life for you. Do you know that? You work so hard and finally have the money you need so you don't have to live like we used to … that may be okay for you, but it's not for me. I'm moving forward and getting out of here. I'll find a place after I get back. In the meantime, I'll stay with Tristan or Darius or maybe even in a hotel, but *this*—" I wave my hands around the room. "I can't take this anymore." I throw some more clothes into a suitcase, grab my purse and a bookbag, and make my way to work.

At this point, I don't even care that I didn't say anything to Carina. She left the conversation. *She* quit on me. I call a driver and show up to the showroom with all my bags.

Tristan is stocking a shelf of ties in a glass display

case. He looks down at my pile of luggage. "I thought you weren't leaving for another week."

"I need to move out. I'm going to get a hotel or something before I leave, and then I'll try to find a place when I get back."

"You're going to live in a hotel? That's nonsense. You can crash with me. You should be no more than what . . . a month?"

"Yeah, I just need this week before fashion week, and then a couple of weeks when I get back."

"Yeah, that's no problem at all. I can get a room ready for you by tomorrow if you don't mind spending tonight in a hotel."

"I don't mind at all."

I take my things upstairs, and Olivia greets me with a confused look. I roll my eyes at her and keep moving until I get to my desk. I definitely don't have the time to deal with whatever it is *she* has to say. I glance over at her desk to see a smug smile on her face. The sound of her heels gets closer and closer to my desk. I don't want to look at her.

"'Can I help you, Olivia? I'm not in the mood."

"You're all ready for fashion week?"

"Why do you care?"

She shrugs. "Eh, you know. Trying to make conversation."

"I don't trust you." I grab my notebooks that are near her and move them to the other side of my desk.

I then proceed to move everything that is on the side that she's on to the other side of my desk.

"Aren't you tired of fighting?"

"I was just getting started."

"Oh. C'mon Sydney. I was just doing a little freshman hazing. I'm sure you would've done it to me if the roles were reversed."

"Actually, no."

I sit there in complete amazement of the person I'm talking to. *Is she bipolar? Should I call the cops?*

"So, fashion week. You're excited?"

"Yeah," I say with all reluctancy. Navigating this conversation is like walking on eggshells while wondering which one will crack. *What is she up to?*

"So, I heard Nicholas and you have been getting close, huh?"

"You *heard*?"

"Well, yeah. You know . . . it's a small circle."

Note to self: never tell anyone anything. Get a journal.

"Nicholas and I have been on a few dates."

"That's sweet. You know he and I used to date back in the day."

"Okay, Olivia, cut the act. What's really going on?"

"There is no act." She puts on an innocent face like a kid unsure of what's going on. "I realize that you're not like the other people who worked here. It looks like you're definitely staying around for the long haul. So, I thought why not get to know you."

"And how do you expect me to believe that when you've been nothing but the Ice Swan since I've gotten here?"

Olivia bites her bottom lip as the side of her mouth goes up. "About that. Let's let bygones be bygones, huh?"

Is she serious right now? I quickly scan my inbox, put some consultations on my calendar, all the while ignoring Olivia, hoping she'd get the hint and slither back to her own desk.

"Oh yeah, your new assistant starts today."

"Assistant? I have an assistant?"

"Yeah Ms. Boss Lady. You are the head stylist now, so you get an assistant."

Whoa.

Olivia and I keep up a conversation for five minutes, and as awkward as it was, I found it refreshing. I've missed having a girlfriend to talk about the stresses and perks that come with this job, like all of the handsome men I get to meet ... but honestly, all I can think about is Nicholas. He's moved our dinner date up to tomorrow night instead of the night before I leave. He says there's something he wants to tell me.

The rest of the day goes by in a blur as my upcoming conversation with Nicholas consumes my thoughts.

My assistant is a sweet, young girl named Camille. And by young, I mean she's about four years younger than me. She's fresh out of college.

I wish I could've had a job like this fresh out of college. I could've been Camille. Well, I shouldn't rush to say that. *Let's see what she's capable of first.*

I started her off with Fashion Week assignments: confirming my attendance for certain shows, RSVPing on my behalf for afterparties, scheduling fittings and meetings ... it seems that I'm going to be spending an entire week in each city while I'm there, averaging between two to three shows a day. Camille is coming with me along with a make-up artist and a hair stylist.

Mr. Barnes and I have a meeting to discuss some key contacts that I'm to meet throughout my travels.

Toward the end of the day, I make plans to have dinner at Tristan's with Darius. He lives in the historic area of Center City called Old City. He's done well for himself and has his own townhome on a cobble-stoned street of colonial homes. His place is definitely a bachelor pad with browns, grays, and blacks all over. His kitchen is modern with a white marble countertop, brown cabinets, and stainless-steel appliances. His dining table is a big slab of dark brown wood held up by brass legs.

"When do you head out?" Darius asks as he pours glasses of wine. Up until this point, I never knew Darius was capable of wearing anything other than a suit. Tonight, he's wearing a pair of dark blue khaki pants with a gray, ribbed sweater, and white sneakers.

"Look at you not in a suit," I say with a smile.

"Oh, stop it," he says playfully as he sets up the rest of the table with white plates and silverware.

"Is this a special occasion or something?"

"Of course. We have a new head stylist who's about to go out of the United States for the first time in her life, experiencing Fashion Week in all of the major international cities. I think that's worth celebrating, don't you?"

I smile as I put both of my elbows on the table to hold up my head. As I lose two friends, it's like I'm gaining two more. I've told Tristan and Darius everything that's been going on with Carina, Corey, and me, omitting all of the backstory, of course.

Darius already had an idea of what was going on since Memorial Day when he witnessed the fight the three of us had as he and I were leaving. I felt so embarrassed that day, but Darius never brought it up..

Tristan places a steaming lasagna in the middle of the table, a big wooden bowl of salad, and a basket of bread. I bow my head to pray but then realize that the men got quiet. *Oh wait, I guess I don't have to if I don't won't to.*

"Sorry, force of habit."

"No, it's cool," Tristan says as he grabs the spatula. We all fill our plates and our glasses.

I opt out of praying and look at my two friends with a smile. This is my life. These are my friends. They are my new family.

"I think a toast is appropriate," Tristan says with his glass raised. "To new beginnings."

"To new beginnings," Darius and I say in unison.

To new beginnings, indeed.

PART TWO

"I said to myself, "Come on, let's try pleasure. Let's look for the 'good things' in life." But I found that this too, was meaningless."

—ECCLESIASTES 2:1

CHAPTER ELEVEN

OCTOBER 1ST

Walking to my desk at Luke and Barnes this Monday morning, I feel so alive. I'm wearing a pair of black Chanel heels that was gifted to me with a black Versace suit, also gifted. I made so many contacts during fashion week—SJH was in full effect. Could I help that people were drawn to me?

The Head Stylist of Luke and Barnes made connections with celebrities for future campaigns. Buyers and merchandisers wanted first dibs on our new arrivals. People wanted *me* to have first dibs on *their* new arrivals. It was such a rush. I was in high demand. People cared about my opinion. They liked me. They wanted me. And I loved every minute of it.

I didn't think about Corey or Carina once ... well, except for the time when I went by the Eiffel Tower, and the time I went to Big Ben. Those were two places Corey and Carina always wanted to visit. But I had to brush those thoughts aside. My life has changed, and I have to leave the old baggage behind

Nicholas managed to meet me while I was in Paris, and we had the most romantic dinner where we made our relationship official. We've been texting every day and meeting for dinners as often as we can. We're both so busy, but I'm happy we're able to make it work.

While I was away, I had a great idea of documenting my time in all four cities: New York, London, Paris, and Milan. I also took the liberty of sending out some email blasts and doing some blog posts. I was able to get into the analytics and found that our site traffic increased by sixty percent—all thanks to me, of course.

Milan was absolutely my favorite. I was more excited about Paris, but the beautiful streets of Milan took my breath away, and that's aside from the Gucci and Botega Veneta shows that had me drooling. I went through my whole box of business cards and added at least one hundred contacts to my phone. I barely got any sleep between the shows and parties, and I lived on caffeine and croissants—not a bad way to live.

My team that went with me were phenomenal and handled all of my looks for the shows and afterparties. Camille was a gem. Definitely worth her stock. She's going to make something of herself in this business for sure. Her extremely organized work ethic has the insane ability to anticipate needs I didn't even know I had.

As I get to my desk, I can see the steam still rising from a cup of coffee, or I should say latte. Lattes have been my one and only drink as of late. Well, I shouldn't say that. I've also been getting into champagnes, and wines, and cocktails. What have I been missing? Drinking was one thing I was always sure I would never get into.

But leave it to Paris to be the one to introduce me to the world of wine: in the evening at a restaurant for an exclusive dinner. Out comes a bottle of red wine everybody said I *had* to try. Red wine was an acquired taste, but by the end of the week, I acquired it alright. It became my drink of choice for dinner. White wine was my drink at lunch, and I had cocktails in between.

Getting to my computer, I see the number on my email inbox in the thousands. I was so busy on the social media kick that I didn't even bother to check my email. The first email I open has no subject and contains a picture ... actually, a couple of pictures.

A picture of Olivia and Nicholas.

What in the world?

The two of them are sitting outside a restaurant laughing. As I scroll down, the second picture shows them leaning in and smiling. In the third picture, Nicholas has his arm around Olivia. The fourth picture—my breath becomes short.

Nicholas and Olivia are kissing.

When did this happen?

I breathe slowly to stop my growing heart rate and hear a familiar set of heels walk into the room.

"Oh, you're back," Olivia says. "How was fashion week, girlfriend?"

I close my eyes and continue breathing slowly. I hear her heels getting closer and a familiar scented mixture of floral and fruity.

"You okay?"

Her hip is leaning on the side of my desk as I open one eye to make sure that nothing of mine is touching her.

The audacity.

Wait, why should I get mad? I knew this was coming. Olivia has had it out for me since the beginning. I know I belong here. I refuse to allow her to make me think otherwise. I know what I'm capable of; the great thing is that she doesn't.

All I've done was play nice. Well, not anymore. I go through my list of contacts that I got from fashion week. It's time to make some calls. Why get mad when I can get even?

* * *

Nicholas and I meet for lunch at Parc since it's the closest place to my office that I like. As soon as we're seated, I glare at him and keep staring at him when I drink from my water glass, and as I eat my piece of bread. All the while, I'm wondering what's going on in his head.

"What's going on? Everything okay?"

He's looking especially handsome today. But I shake off what could eventually weaken my stance. I need him to see that I'm serious and am not to be messed with.

"You tell me, Nicholas. Is there anything going on? You know, I thought everything was fine when we left Paris. I guess not." I grab my napkin and put it across my lap. This is going to require another piece of bread—and extra butter.

"Okay, Syd, what's going on?"

"Don't call me Syd."

His face scrunches up as he takes a drink from his water glass.

"I got a picture today in my email."

"Okay," he says, motioning with his hand to keep going.

"The picture had two people in it that I was surprised to see."

"Sydney just come out with it already."

No, you're going to take this.

"It was two people who I thought were over, finished. Honestly, I even forgot they were ever together." Slowly sipping my water, I watch as he rubs his hand over his hair. "So, what kind of stuff did you get into while I was away? Or better yet... *who*?" My voice gets louder. "How dare you come to Paris and start a relationship to only days later go back to what you had."

"What are you talking about?"

"You and Olivia! You know she hates me. I've told you what it's been like working with her. Yet, here you go, smiling and hugging and kissing on her."

"I never did any of that."

The server comes over, and I burst out into laughter. We place our order, and I find that I can't stop laughing.

"Do you think I'm a fool? Nicholas, I have pictures." My voice hasn't lowered, and he begins to look at the other people around us.

"There's no need to consider other people's feelings now. You weren't doing that when you were here with Olivia."

I show him the picture and I see his jaw clench. He rubs both hands over his head and then brings his chair next to mine. He puts his arm around me. As much as I want to tear away, there's something comforting about his arm being there. I lay my head on his shoulder as my ears start to burn. My chest hurts as I try to swallow as hard as I can so that the tears that are forming don't fall out of my eyes. I don't want to lose the first relationship I've ever been in. Who would've thought a guy like Nicholas—handsome, rich, smooth—who could get any woman he wanted, would end up with someone like me?

"Sydney, what I can promise you is that any feelings towards Olivia are completely gone. I wouldn't hop on a plane to Paris for just anybody." His voice became lower and gentle. He puts his head on top of mine and takes a few deep breaths. After a while, our breathing patterns synchronize, and I turn to look at him.

"You really are over her?"

"Like I said, I don't get on a plane to Paris for just anybody."

He kisses my cheek and puts his head back on top of mine.

"I know it's been stressful with your new role and trying to move. Why don't we go out to dinner tonight?" he says.

"Darius and Tristan are putting something together for my birthday. I guess you could come," I say with a sad face.

He chuckles.

My head still resting on his shoulder, I close my eyes and see images of us in Paris flash through my mind. Us going from party to party with no care in the world. The amazing dinners that we had at world-class restaurants.

Not on my watch.

She won't win that easy. I won't let her.

Speaking of Olivia …

* * *

All I received from Tristan was a text with an address telling me where to meet him for dinner and to text him when I get there. I'm assuming this is my birthday dinner … at least I hope so. As I approach the building, I recognize it as the same place I went to for my meeting with Mr. Barnes. Tristan told me to wear something really nice, so I put on a little black dress that is form fitting and comes down just below my knees. I throw on a pair of black heels and a red lip, and I looked like I was never at work.

As the elevator door opened, Nicholas is standing there with a bouquet of roses.

"Happy Birthday, babe." He kisses me on the lips.

"So, it is my birthday dinner!" I say. I smile wide as I take his arm and walk to our table. Actually, we don't have a table; we have a private room! Darius and Tristan are standing as I walk in, dressed in nice three-pieced suits.

"Happy Birthday!" Tristan and Darius say in unison.

"Thank you, guys!" I smile and for a moment expect Carina and Corey to show up.

Old baggage, remember?

I shake my head to shake away the thoughts of the past and embrace my new life.

Nicholas pulls out my chair as I place the bouquet of roses he gave me in the middle of the table. A server comes over to fill my water glass.

I take my seat at our table and realize I'm the only woman here. Without Carina and Corey, my only real friends are Darius, Tristan, and Nicholas. I didn't think this year would bring new friendships. But I can't think about that right now. It's time to celebrate. Glasses of wine sparkle all around the table, but what catches my eye is a small gold box with a red ribbon on top waiting for me at my place setting.

"You guys! This is so nice, I've never done anything like this before." I can't tell them it's because I couldn't afford it. Normally, Corey, Carina, and I would get cheesesteaks or pizza and a cake and binge watch *Dorian Gray*. Other times we've gone to an amusement park. But dressing up? This is what I really wanted. And it's happening with Tristan, Darius, and Nicholas. This is the first time I'm not spending my birthday with Carina and Corey since we've known each other. Although it feels different, it feels good.

My phone buzzes, and I look down to see a missed call and voicemail from Carina. There's a text, a missed call, and a voicemail from Corey as well.

I excuse myself and head to the restroom. The restroom has stalls that have full doors like in a house, so I take the stall toward the end and sit on the cover of the toilet. Hearing Carina's voice as I listen to her message brings a pain to my chest I wasn't' ready for. I can feel tears beginning to come, and I don't even try to stop them this time.

The tears come harder as I'm listening to Corey's message. I miss his voice. There's so much care and warmth in its rasp. My stomach begins to ache as the cries come harder and harder. I begin to think about all the mean things Olivia has said to me, the fights that I've had with Corey and Carina, the lack of sleep I've had these past few months, the picture of Nicholas and Olivia …

All of that comes to a head as I flip the toilet seat up and release the lunch I ate earlier. The release happens for another five minutes, and I sit on the toilet with my hand in my head. *I have to clean myself up. It's your birthday, Sydney. You have a gorgeous man out there and two good friends ready to celebrate you in the most wonderful restaurant. Get it together.*

I dab my face with toilet tissue as I prepare to see myself in the mirror. My red lipstick is all over my chin, and my mascara has run down both cheeks. I try to fix it as much as I can with the concealer, mascara, and red lipstick that I brought, but the damage is evident. I take a deep breath as I walk out of the restroom. I hold my head high, but I feel an emptiness in the pit of my stomach that won't seem to go away.

CHAPTER TWELVE

NOVEMBER 12TH

It's moving day. After a few weeks, I was finally able to find the perfect place at The Atlantic. I used to walk by the place a lot and dream of the life the people who live there had, and now I get to be one of those people. Tristan, Darius, and Nicholas are helping me.

Waiting for the elevator for our third trip up, out pops a familiar face wearing her signature bun.

"Olivia?"

Her default frown remains as she removes her sunglasses.

"What are *you* doing here?" she says, looking me over.

Ah, now that's the Olivia I remember.

"I'm moving in," I say with a smile of satisfaction. Her eyes scan the three men who are with me and the bins and boxes we're about to load onto the elevator. She walks away without saying anything, and my mind begins to replay all the phone calls I made to all of the contacts from Fashion Week. Some of them were actually clients of Olivia. Not for long.

Once we get to my new apartment, we put the boxes and bins in the middle of my living room. I still can't believe I'm living here. I go to one of the three floor-to-ceiling windows in the living room that overlooks Love Park and gives a glimpse of the Art Museum—the place where this all started. I turn back around to face my modern digs: marble counters in the kitchen, stainless steel appliances, a huge rainfall shower ... *this*, this is living.

As we go back downstairs for our last trip of the move, I realize that I left something at my desk at work.

* * *

"What do you think you're doing?" Olivia asks as she stands by the side of my desk with her hand on her hip.

"I'm sorry, do we have an appointment? You can speak to my assistant to schedule a meeting if you need to talk."

Tristan walks in with a messenger bag across his black suit.

"You stole my contacts," Olivia says bitterly.

"Again, you need to speak to my—"

"I have voice messages of people telling me that they've enjoyed our time together, but they want you as their stylist. What the heck did you do?"

Her tone was harsh, and her word choice, harsher as she throws out curses at me.

"I don't know what you're talking about." I try to keep a smile from forming as I go through the folders on my desk. Olivia gets closer as she curses even more which prompts me to stand up.

Tristan jogs over and gets in between us. "Whoa, whoa, whoa ladies. Let's not do this. C'mon. To your corners."

Olivia and I don't break eye contact as she walks backward to her desk.

I slowly sit down at mine. *The nerve of her! If she would do her job like everybody claims she's so good at, people wouldn't need to switch, now would they?*

"You were just helping me move, how did you get here so fast? And in a suit?" I say.

"The bigger question is what's going on between y'all," Tristan says as he sits down at his desk.

"What *hasn't* been going on, Tristan?" I ask with more bite in my tone. "Somebody finally beat her at her own game."

"This isn't a game," Olivia says as she puts files in her drawers. "This is real life. And you better learn that fast before someone gets hurt." She grabs her coat and her purse and walks out of the office.

I roll my eyes, check a few emails, and get up to leave.

"Be careful, Sydney. You don't want to mess with her."

"She doesn't want to mess *me*. Whose side are you on anyway?"

"It's not about sides, Syd, it's about—"

"Don't call me Syd." For some reason, Tristan calling me Syd in that moment reminds me of Corey. "And, of course, it's about sides. I've told you everything that's been going on between her and me, and you have the nerve to tell *me* to chill?" I shake my head. "I'll see you at the silent auction tonight." I leave the office with my ears hotter than normal and my face heating up. I hate that instead of punching something or screaming, my body responds to anger through tears. But here comes the Nile River once again.

* * *

Leave it to me to schedule a move on the same day that I have to attend another gala—I managed to only be fifteen minutes late. The trumpet player in the jazz band is performing a solo as I walk into the ballroom of the Loews Hotel. We're on the thirty-third floor which offers panoramic views of the Philadelphia skyline. It's my favorite thing to see at night. All the lights from different buildings lighting up the sky. I love watching people maneuvering through crowded sidewalks amongst lighted trees. This is my city.

As a congratulations for moving into my own place, I bought myself a necklace with earrings to match from Tiffany's that I thought would be perfect to debut with my muted-gold ball gown and matching shoes tonight. My first pieces of jewelry from Tiffany's, and I was able to buy it myself as the Head Stylist of Luke + Barnes. This time last year I was working at that French café near the showroom. I haven't been in there lately; maybe I should stop by for a visit.

I look around and wave at all of the familiar faces from the polo game and some from Fashion Week. But I don't see three faces in particular.—Nicholas, Darius, and Tristan.

Fewer tables are set up for this function than were at the Christmas gala, but it's still as grand. The Philadelphia skyline acts as the backdrop for the six, crystal chandeliers hanging from the ceiling. A small dancing area is set up in front of the band.

Mr. Barnes puts on the silent auction every year to raise money for his non-profit, *The Barnes Foundation*. that provides clothes for people who can't afford professional attire for the workplace.

I notice they didn't assign seats for this event, except for Mr. Barnes' table, which is right in front of the dance floor and has the most elaborate centerpiece of all the tables in the room. Orange, red, and yellow flowers spill over the vase that's probably as high my waist.

I take a seat with my back to the door so I can stare into the night sky. I finally have a place to myself. It's in The Atlantic. I have the job of my dreams and the man of my dreams, yet here I am, sitting by myself at a Luke and Barnes event. There's a familiar ache in my stomach that is returning. I put my elbows on the table to prop up my head with my hands. Interlocking my fingers together, I close my eyes.

This is what I wanted. This is truly life. I'm finally living.

Then why do I feel so empty inside?

"Hello, beautiful."

I open my eyes and kiss Nicholas as he sits next to me in his classic tuxedo. His hair is slicked back, and the scent of his woodsy cologne tickles my nose. But I can sense another scent mixed in. *Is that a floral scent?* I casually get closer to Nicholas and sniff as silently as I can without coming off like a weirdo. A hint of something both floral and fruity is in his scent this evening. A scent that I've smelled once before.

A lump forms in my throat as I wave for a server to refill my water glass. That familiar pang in my stomach has returned. I want to bend over, but I save face and manufacture a smile I hope is convincing, especially to me. Out of the corner of my left eye, I see

Olivia walk in with a slim, burnt-orange gown that leaves a small train behind her. Her neckline is lower than how she usually wears her dresses. I watch her as she looks around the room. Her gaze finds mine and that smug smile returns to the corner of her mouth. She walks toward my table, and I can feel my ears getting hotter and hotter.

"Nicholas, how are you doing?"

Nicholas clears his throat. "Olivia."

"Sydney, it's nice to see you this evening."

I remain silent. I squint at her at her as she walks away to find another table. She talks with some of the people I remember from Fashion Week and glances back at me a few times, smiling and laughing.

Mr. Barnes walks in with about ten people in front of him and ten people behind him. Olivia makes herself one of the first people to greet him once he arrives. Her conversation with him seems longer than normal as she glances my way. So does Mr. Barnes.

What is she talking to him about?

Olivia walks over to my table and mentions that Mr. Barnes wants to speak with me. She walks behind me to where Mr. Barnes is, and he motions for both of us to follow him.

We find a seating area in front of the restrooms as Mr. Barnes offers his hand for the two of us to sit down.

"Olivia, you tell me that Sydney took all of your clients?"

"All of my clients called me and said that they now want to work with Sydney." Olivia managed to act hurt and surprised.

"And how do you know that it was Sydney's fault. From what I can see, Sydney has been doing more for the brand than you have. She's been taking initiative on social media which is something you never did when I sent you to Fashion Week. She's made meaningful connections at both the polo game and Fashion week. She takes risk. I don't see the problem here."

"The problem is that she spoke with my clients without my permission and convinced them to all be with her."

Mr. Barnes looks at me.

"I can't help that I'm good at what I do, Mr. Barnes." I innocently shrug. "That's why you hired me."

Mr. Barnes looks at me and then at Olivia.

"Olivia, suck it up. This is business. This isn't high school. Now get clients on your books soon or there won't be a need for you to get clients at all without a job. As for you, Ms. Humphries, you never cease to amaze me. I want to make you my Director of Styling. I want you to be in charge of both Tristan and Olivia."

I glance at Olivia, and the shocked look on her face was priceless.

Checkmate.

No longer can Olivia try to walk all over me in thousand-dollar boots. She works for *me* now. I run this ship. I take a small but deep breath in as I inhale my new position and exhale the old. A smile forms on my face as an image of my new business cards flash in my mind: Sydney Humphries, Director of Styling.

And the pay increase! I try to keep my composure just thinking of all of the new things I'll be able to get: a bigger apartment, fancier dinners, another bump up in wardrobe. I could even get a car. There's no need to drive it anywhere, but at least I can say I have one. Oh, and I can get a driver. This is going to be fun.

"You have fresh perspective," Mr. Barnes continues, "a passion for the brand, and new momentum that will carry us very far. We'll talk about it at the top of the new year, but be on the lookout for some paperwork coming your way. Now, you ladies enjoy the evening and give generously; that's why we're here."

Mr. Barnes leaves, and I stand up to follow him back to ballroom, deserting Olivia to dust the smoke off of the backfire that just occurred.

Smiling as I return to the event, I find Tristan and Darius sitting at the table.

"Hey, is everything okay?" Tristan asks, looking at Mr. Barnes and then at me.

"Oh yeah," I say. "Everything is perfect. In fact, you're looking at the new Director of Styling."

Tristan's face scrunches from a look of concern into confusion.

"Director? We don't even have that position."

"Mr. Barnes just created it for me. He said he loves my passion for the brand and my risk-taking. I'll be starting in the new year."

Tristan's mouth curls down as he looks off in another direction.

"Aren't you happy for me?" I say, smiling as I sit down.

Olivia abruptly comes up to me as soon as I grab my water glass.

"Look, I don't know what kind of games you're playing, little orphan Annie, but this is the big leagues. Mr. Barnes is not your Daddy Warbucks, and neither is Nicholas." She turns to Nicholas. "It was nice seeing you earlier. I hope we could do it again."

She turns back to me. "You thought you could do what you did in high school, didn't you?"

I clench my jaw and narrow my eyes. *Who told her about—*

"Oh yeah. Corey told me. We had a nice little conversation while you were away. He was feeling so sad with no one to talk to, so, of course, when I gave the invitation to join me for lunch he jumped at the chance—"

"Olivia, what are you doing?" Tristan asks.

"Oh, Tristan, don't you see? Our little orphan girl was trying to play grown up. She didn't realize that unlike high school, grown-ups bite back " She turns to me. "And don't you forget it." She walks away.

A tear forms in the corner of my eye. I close my eyes as I hear the taunts again. As I see the people gathering around me in my mind, pointing at me, laughing at me. They said that I could never be anything more than what I was.

What *was* I? Just a girl who grew up without her parents. Raised by her grandmother in her one-bedroom apartment. A girl who tried to make the best of every situation. I tried to patch holes over everything, but the seam ripped. I walked into the halls on the first day of freshman year thinking it was a clean slate, but everything came back to haunt me. I thought I could create a new image—the girl with cool clothes that everybody wanted to be around—yet nobody would actually be my friend.

All I had was Corey and Carina. Carina was on the cheerleading team, and Corey was on the football team, and I was a sack of potatoes—dead weight. What was I really good for then?

I got the nickname of "Annie" in my high school because of my curly hair, it rang even more true once people found out that I was an orphan. My grandmother did the best she could, but she couldn't heal the wounds of the words spoken at me during school.

On graduation day, sitting on the stage as the guest speaker gave her speech, I thought about what my life was getting ready to look like being in Connecticut for four years, and that's when I made the vow to myself. *I will come out on top.* And it rings true now as much as it did then.

I will still come out on top.

CHAPTER THIRTEEN

DECEMBER 13TH

One year later. I'm back at the Art Museum in the ballroom that forever changed my life. I survey the room from right to left. I now know mostly all of the people here. My dress is bigger. It's a red, princess ball gown that comes off the shoulder with a sweetheart neckline. I'm wearing the same jewelry that I wore for the silent auction. Only a year ago, I was here with Corey aweing at the opulence.

My stomach pangs with the thought of Corey. I haven't spoken to them at all. I never returned their call from my birthday. It's best that way. They'll go their own way, and I'll go mine. They'll see what it is they're missing and will want to join me. They'll see the error of their ways.

I find my spot at Mr. Barnes' table and wait for Nicholas to arrive. He said he had some last-minute work conflicts to resolve.

The jazz band roars a lively rendition of "We Wish You a Merry Christmas" as a server fills my water glass. Ten minutes goes by, and none of my friends—Tristan, Darius, and Nicholas—have shown up. A slight pang forms in my stomach again. I rest both of my arms on my lap.

I am all you need.

"Huh?" I say out loud at hearing a soft voice like a whisper. I definitely heard it in my left ear, so I turn around, but no one's behind me.

Sydney, I am all you need.

Fear wraps its hands around my neck. I won't let anything mess up this moment. This is my time to shine. I wouldn't be surprised if Mr. Barnes decides to announce my promotion tonight. Actually, this would be a great night to do it. I'm going to suggest it.

There's no need to run away from me. I have always loved you.

I turn my head both ways and still find nobody behind me. *This can't be happening.*

"No, no, no, no, no," I say with my head in my hands. "Why? Why tonight?" The voice speaks with so much love, it's terrifying.

I didn't hear the voice for the rest of the night, but what I remember most is that the voice was filled with love. Which is weird. I never heard those words or felt those words as I have in that instant—not even from Nicholas. *Where is he?* Did I miss the memo here? Is everybody coming late on purpose?

Come back to me. I am all you need.

"Leave me alone!" I say to no one. People begin to look at me as I'm still at a table by myself. My eyes begin to well up with tears as I let my head drop into my hands. *Nope, not tonight. Tonight is my night to shine.* A warm hand touches my bare shoulder, and I turn around to see Nicholas standing in a midnight-blue tuxedo. His hair is gone.

"You cut your hair!" I exclaim.

It's short on the sides and the back and longer in the front. We hug and kiss, and I wrap my arms around him and hold on for dear life. *This is my dream. I'm living my dream.* I touch my Tiffany earrings and necklace and smooth down my dress. *I'm living my dream.* I look around at all of the people who are now familiar to me.

I'm living my dream.

PART THREE

"Those who have money will never have enough.
How meaningless to think that wealth
brings true happiness!"

—ECCLESIASTES 5:10

CHAPTER FOURTEEN

FEBRUARY 2ND

Even as my life continues to go up into a new stratosphere, *something* always brings me down. This time: Olivia is coming with me for Fashion Week. I'm supposed to show her the method to my madness when it comes to social media marketing and stuff. I guess it couldn't be all bad. She'll be able to get a front-row seat to the amazingness that is her new Director of Styling. Now that I think about it, I'm *her* immediate supervisor now. Oh, this could be interesting.

* * *

The flood of yellow taxi cabs greets me as my train pulls into New York City. Olivia decided to fly… which is crazy because NYC is only two hours away from Philly. Camille takes care of my check-in, and I go straight up to my room because we have T-minus two hours before we have to attend Michale Kors' show. We're in the same suite in the same hotel I stayed in last year—The Designer Suite at the St. Regis Hotel. The room offers a perfect fusion of classic and modern style of furniture and fabrics in the bedroom and living room.

We unpack and set up my clothes in the living room on tall, silver, clothing racks and put shoes under each outfit. While the makeup artist is attending to my face, a nail tech I've hired gives me a manicure every day. Today we're going with a classic French manicure We'll see what inspires me tomorrow. My first show is Michael Kors and then it's off to Carolina Herrara and then Coach.

I haven't checked in with Olivia, I'm going to let my assistant deal with that. As I'm getting fitted for my outfit for the Michael Kors show, someone knocks at the door. Camille opens it and tells Olivia to come into the living room.

"Olivia," I say, keeping my gaze ahead.

"Is there something that I should know or something you need to tell me before we go to this show?" Olivia says with an attitude

I've never heard such disgust in her voice before. Ha! I let the moment linger in silence. I begin to give her a run-down of the different social media platforms I use while Camille gives her visual demonstrations.

"Unlike what you're used to, we need to be on time for these things," I say. The hairstylist is putting the finishing touches on my hair—bone-straight with front bangs. I like it. I think I'll wear my hair like this more often. Straightened, my hair comes down below my shoulder blades. It's a mix of dark brown and black that I never really appreciated until now.

Looking in the mirror over the dresser, I'm obsessed with the blush tones and neutral eyeshadows that my makeup artist chose for today. I think it compliments my tan Michael Kors dress and black boots perfectly. Camille hands me my sunglasses and drapes my floor-length, brown fur coat across my shoulders.

"You have my latte?" I ask Camille.

"Yes, your caramel latte is right here." She holds up a paper cup.

"Let's do this." I grab my latte and walk out of the room with as much fierceness as Naomi Campbell down a runway. Olivia and I ride in an Escalade together, and I look over her social media posts before she puts them up. We barely speak to each other while both of us are on our phones. I wouldn't have it any other way.

* * *

Returning to the hotel, Camille tells Olivia of the schedule for the evening.

"We have to catch an early flight tomorrow. How long are we going to be at this party?" Olivia asks

"I'm not sure, but an RSVP has been sent on your behalf already, so your attendance would be expected."

Olivia rolls her eyes and takes the first elevator that opens.

Now I see why she is where she is, and I am where I am.

Entering into my room, I kick off my heels and leave them by the door. A tray of food is sitting on the coffee table with a silver cloche on top. I realize I'm famished.

You're filling up on the wrong things.

I turn my head to look toward my clothing rack where Camille and the hairdresser are working on my look for tonight.

"Camille, did you say something?"

"No, no I didn't. You enjoy your lunch." She smiles and resumes her conversation.

I open the silver dome and find a delectable turkey club sandwich with avocado, bacon, and a side of fries. I clap my hands with as much excitement as a kid who just received permission to eat a cookie before dinner.

As a fry is in mid-flight into my mouth, I hear, *You've been eating on the wrong things. They won't fill you up.*

I put the fry down and walk over to Camille and my hair stylist.

"You're sure you didn't say something?" I say as I grab her shoulders.

"I'm sure, Sydney, I promise. We just finalized a look for you for this evening. What do you think about—"

I am all that you need.

"Ha!" I spin around and put up my hands, prepared to fight whatever or whoever is behind me.

Wait.

That voice ... that voice that comes from ... from somewhere ... I slowly walk back to the sofa and flop down.

"No, not again!" I put my head in my hands as I recall what took place a couple months ago at the Christmas gala.

I am all you need. There's something about this voice. It triggers a well of emotions that makes me want to scream in anger, cry in sadness, and laugh in joy all at the same time.

"No, not right now. Please, not right now. I'm about to go to this awesome party, and I can't have this voice chasing me all the way there." I hit my head a few times with my hands.

"Is everything okay, Sydney? Is there something wrong with your food?"

"No, Camille. Everything is fine," I say with a sigh.

I slide down the couch until my upper back is the only thing that's holding me up. *Why is this happening*

— 156 —

to me? I let myself slide the rest of the way to the floor and eat my fries. A few tears escape from the corners of my eyes, and I quickly grab a tissue before the Nile River flows. *Nope, not right now, not today.*

I pick up a fry to eat, but then throw it aimlessly on my plate as if I could throw away this voice.

I am all you need.

I hold both hands to my ears and scream to shut out all of the noise.

Camille and the hair stylist look at me with their mouths open.

"Sydney—"

"I'm fine!" I shove the table away from me, spilling something on the floor. Walking into the bedroom, I slam the door and jump unto my bed. I'm sure makeup is probably on the pillow, but at this point I don't care. Maybe closing my eyes will make everything go away. But every time there's even five minutes of silence, a brief memory reveals itself from high school.

This time, the memory isn't from high school. My grandmother is at the table with Corey and Carina sitting on either side of me. It's after church, and Grandma has made an awesome lunch.

"What did you guys learn in Children's Church today?"

"Samuel!"

We all scream in unison. Our teachers always made a point to make the lessons interactive and memorable. They had us act as if we were sleeping and whisper our names while we couldn't see them.

"That's one of my favorite stories," my grandmother says as she puts a forkful of salad into her mouth.

"Samuel was probably your age when God started talking to him."

"Can we talk to God, Grandma?" Carina asks

"Absolutely, you can," she says with a smile. "In fact, he's waiting for you to talk to him. Even more, he wants to talk to you."

"I want God to talk to me, Grandma," I say.

"I'm sure he will, sweetheart. You just have to promise me one thing. Promise me that you will listen and answer when he does."

"I promise."

My eyes slowly open in my hotel room and I can feel clumps of mascara mixing with my tears. I inhale the typical hotel smell of the pillow and let out a wail from the depths of my stomach. More pangs form in my stomach as I grab my phone from the nightstand. Scrolling down my contacts, I come across Carina's name. I know her phone number by heart. My thumb hovers over the call button, but I can't bring myself to press it.

I'm fine. I'm living my dream.

I throw my phone to the other side of my king-sized bed and rush into the bathroom to take off the eye makeup. *The makeup artist will just have to do it again.*

Camille is typing furiously on her laptop when I go back into the living room. She quickly closes her computer and stands up.

"Is everything okay? Is there anything I can get you?"

I flop onto the couch with a heavy sigh.

"Get Clarissa back in here to touch up my makeup. And get a ginger ale. Oh, and an aspirin."

Camille immediately leaves, and the room goes quiet. I jump up from the sofa.

"Alright," I say to a quiet room, "look, *God*, if it really is you … this is so stupid. I'm talking to air. I'm literally talking to air."

I flop back onto the couch and kick my feet like a seven-year-old having a tantrum.

"I just need to survive these next few cities."

CHAPTER FIFTEEN

JANUARY 24TH

"The coffee here even tastes better!" Camille yelps as she gets back into the car.

We made a stop at a café to refuel from a red-eye to Paris. I stare out of the window the entire trip to our hotel. It's a different kind of bustle here, not like the hustle and grind of American business culture. This is a hubbub in living life. People actually *living*.

What does that feel like?

The few shows we go to are all a blur. My head hurts from the lack of sleep on the plane. I don't even want to think about all of the parties I'll be going to tonight. Four parties, four different outfits, one exhausted Sydney.

When I return to my hotel room, I find a turkey club under a cloche on a tray on the coffee table.

Déjà vu.

Nope. This will not happen again. I tear into my meal, slurping down my ginger ale.

"Camille!" I call to her. "Get me a bottle of champagne!"

I stand and look at the rack of clothes. There's one more fashion show to attend—Monte Cristo. The godmother of all fashion, the centuries-old fashion house closes Paris Fashion Week every year. A-list celebrities and even some dignitaries attend Monte Cristo's show. I want to be ready and slightly buzzed. Maybe the alcohol will block the voice.

I squint my eyes at the rack of clothes as an idea begins to form. I rummage through the suitcases and find a needle and thread—my weapon of choice. I grab two dresses off of the rack and work my magic. The paparazzi would eat this up ... and so would the head designer of Monte Cristo, who's going to be there.

This may actually be my chance. It's like riding a bike. I push and pull the needle and thread seamlessly over and under the two dresses. Then I take a swig of champagne from the bottle and furiously poke the needle through the fabrics. I poke myself multiple times, but I refuse to let that stop me. Many minutes go by, but I look at my creation in the mirror and smile. What was once two dresses have now become a jumpsuit. No one will be expecting this.

Many flashes from the cameras of the paparazzi come my way as we walk two blocks to the venue for the fashion show. Camille ushers me inside, and we take our seats—I in the front row, Camille, three rows back—and wait for the show to begin. *Why did we get here so early?* I look down at my jumpsuit, one pants leg turquoise and one yellow with a purple top. And then there's the empty runway. I stare at the white, elevated platform. *I wonder what it would be like to walk the runway.*

No, Sydney, you can't. You're a director right now. You have to act with some decorum. *But we are here pretty early . . .*

I walk towards the back of the room and hoist myself up to the end of the runway. The lights are so bright it's hard to see anyone or anything. *You better start walking before somebody comes!* The wide-legged pants of my jumpsuit softly blow in the wind that I created as I walk.

Once I get to the end of the runway, I place my hand on my hip and pause. Basking in all of the lights.

I can get used to this.

"Sydney, get down!"

I hear Olivia yelling but I can't see her because of all of the lights. I do two more runs up and down the runway and then bow once I reach the end.

As I sit back down in my seat, I let out a sigh of contentment.

"What were you doing up there?" Olivia says angrily.

"Making a statement. You should try it."

"If you don't cut it out, you're going to get us thrown out."

"And if I don't take risks, I'll never know what'll happen. That's why I'm where I am, and that's why you're where you are."

"And what, exactly, do you want to happen?"

I ignore the question, put on my shades, and allow the rest of the seats to fill up.

The Monte Cristo show goes as fast as the bottle of champagne I had delivered to my hotel room this morning.

Camille makes me aware that someone wants to speak with me backstage. *I've never been backstage before. Keep it together, Sydney. Remember, SJH. SJH.*

Backstage, people are running around like chickens with their head cut off, hugging everyone for a job well done, air kisses on both cheeks as greetings, news outlets with their phones in people's faces. *I love it.*

Camille walks me to the person who wanted to—

"There she is!" a male voice says. "There's the person who dared to walk on the runway before its time." This gentleman speaking has his blond hair gelled into a spikey bed on the top of his head. His floral suit has pops of green, pinks, and whites patterned all over. There's only one man who wears the same pink, green, and white suit during the Monte Cristo show every year: it's head designer, Antoine DuBois,

"And what's your name?" he yells into my ear over all of the noise.

"Sydney Jamillah Humphries," I yell back. "This is my assistant, Camille"

"Sydney, so you made a jumpsuit out of two of my dresses? I'm obsessed!"

"I did. And I can do more."

"Let's set up a meeting."

"I'll have my assistant set it up."

We air kiss on both sides, and Camille briefly speaks to Anotine's assistant who is standing right behind him, and then she ushers me into the frigid, New York, winter air.

Getting into the car, I see that Olivia is already in there, waiting on us. I get out my phone and catch up on text messages and emails.

"Don't contact him, Camille."

Her eyes grow wide. "Wait, what?"

"Don't contact him. We can use this as leverage."

Olivia clears her throat.

"Can I help you?" I respond.

"It looks like you can handle this on your own. I don't even know why I'm here."

"I was thinking the same thing."

Once we reach the hotel, Olivia quickly gets out and slams the door, and thankfully, I never see her for the rest of the trip.

CHAPTER SIXTEEN

MARCH 9TH

I tug at my black and white tweed Monte Cristo jacket as I ride the elevator to the fourth floor of the Luke + Barnes store. It's my first time back in the office since my Fashion Week travels.

Camille is already at my desk arranging whatever it is she arranges. My large latte is piping hot as I grab it and take my seat. This is my domain. This is my kingdom. I take my phone and head to the conference room to make a phone call to Mr. Barnes.

"Mr. Barnes, hello, it's Sydney. I understand you're a very busy man, but I realized that you never returned my call from Paris. If you could please give me a call back, I would appreciate it. Thank you."

Mr. Barnes doesn't know what he's missing. I made so many contacts that would help us expand into the European market, so I proposed a bigger pay raise on the way back from Paris. I told him that I had a presentation ready, but I didn't. I just let Camille put it together on the flight. It's only right. I mean, I have the head designer of Monet Cristo as a contact in my phone now. Mr. Barnes should be begging me to stay.

I go back to my desk and find my inbox flooded with emails. I tried to keep up with my email while I was away, but after a while, I didn't care. My clients should know that I'm busy and unavailable during Fashion Week.

The first email opens from one of my clients who—wants to go back to Olivia?

"Camille!" I yell.

She scurries to the side of my desk.

I point to my email.

"What is this?" I watch as Camille focuses on the screen.

"Um, it looks like Mr. Sedville is wanting to go back to Olivia," she says slowly and deliberately with a hint of fear in her voice.

"I know what it says. I'm not stupid. *Why* is he saying this?"

"I don't know Sydney—"

"Don't call me Sydney! Call me Ms. Humphries."

She seems taken aback, but I need to put my foot down. I've been spoiling my staff.

"I can get on the phone and—"

"You do that. And come back immediately once you've found something out."

I cross my arms and sit back in my chair. My phone buzzes, and I don't even bother to look at the caller ID when I answer it.

"Sydney Humphries," I say with as much dryness as the Arizona heat.

"Oh, I'm sorry, is this a bad time?"

I should've looked at the caller ID. I take the phone away from my ear and feel my mouth drop open. It's been months. I've avoided calls and texts, but yet he still calls. Corey still wants to speak with me.

"Hello?" Corey says.

Why would he call now? What could he possibly have to say to me? *I can't deal with this right now.* I quickly end the call and go back to checking my emails. The emails get more and more blurry as tears begin to form in my eyes.

Corey.

"What's going on with Camille?" Tristan says as he walks in. He drops his messenger bag on his chair and walks to my desk. I quickly wipe the few tears from my eyes, grab my compact powder from my desk, and turn around to face Tristan.

"She's doing her job. None of your business."

"Whoa, what's with the ice brigade with that response?"

"Look, if y'all would do your job around here, Camille wouldn't have to be picking up the slack. I can't help it if everyone wants me to be their stylist."

"Um, Ms. Humphries?"

"What?" I quickly turn my head and see Camille standing in the doorway clenching her teeth.

"What is it, Camille? Spit it out," I say as she's walking up to me.

"It looks like as if Olivia has received a brand-new batch of clients."

"'It looks like?' What are you saying? Are telling me Olivia took her clients back?"

"What do you mean *back*?" Tristan interjects.

"None of your business." I put my hand in the direction of his face hoping he gets the message to butt out. This has nothing to do with him. I walk over to the conference room and motion for Camille to go in first.

I close the door behind us. "How did this happen?"

"I don't know, Syd—uh, Ms. Humphries."

"I don't pay you to *not know*, Camille. Find me everything you can on what happened. I want phone calls, emails, text messages—"

"I think that's illegal though."

"Did I ask for your opinion? Do what I say."

If Olivia wants to play hardball, we can play hardball.

As Camille and I leave the conference room, a mixture of familiar scents blows in: woodsy, floral, musk, fruity. Each note detected separately, but when mixed together makes my head scream of pain. I roll my eyes and go to my desk.

"You're late."

Olivia ignores me and sits down at her desk, turning on her computer.

"Excuse me, I said you're late."

She looks at me and then continues to set up her desk for the day.

"I am your boss, and you will treat me with respect."

"I will treat you with respect once you deserve it," she bites back.

Heat rises from the back of my neck to my ears and then spreads around my forehead. *She must think I'm stupid.*

"And how is Nicholas doing?" My arms crossed as I walk closer to her desk.

Her eyes lift up to meet mine, and her mouth opens to speak.

"You're fired," I tell her.

"What? You can't do that."

"Last I checked, I'm *your* boss, so I can do whatever the heck I want to do. Pack your stuff and get up. And tell Nicholas we're done."

I walk to my desk, pick up a notebook, and slam it down. *I need a drink.* I grab my coat and my purse and make my way back home. *There may not be restaurants open now, but Bar de la Sydney is always open.*

* * *

Even with the heat on, my apartment feels colder than usual. I throw my purse and coat across my white-marble countertop and walk directly to my golden bar cart by the window.

The ringer on my phone is going off. *Who could possibly want something now?* I check the phone and find the same name from earlier. The same name that made those pangs come back to my stomach. My mind says no, but my finger presses "Accept."

"Hello?" I say in a hushed tone.

"Humphries."

I refuse to let him know how comforting his voice sounds.

"So, how are you?" he asks. What a loaded question. A simple question, yet I don't quite know how to answer it. *Everybody around me are bums who can barely get anything done.*

"I'm doing okay, I guess."

There's silence for a moment but there's no

awkwardness. My mouth begins to form the words *how are you*, but nothing comes out. More silence fills the air between us—or I should say the airwaves.

"So, are you guys in the playoffs?" I finally say. "Well, I guess not, if you're sitting here talking to me." Immediately, I hit my forehead with the palm of my hand. *Way to go, Sydney.* I mouth the words *I'm sorry* as if he can see me through the phone.

He chuckles and lets out a heavy sigh. "No, we didn't make it. So, everything's going well?"

Well, I guess you don't want to talk about that. It's crazy that we've been friends for almost twenty years, but we can't even say more than ten words to each other.

"I'm a Director of Styling now," I say with pride as I swallow some champagne. *Always come out on top. Always come out on—*

"That's nice," he says.

I take a deep breath and close my eyes. My mind immediately goes back to a memory of Corey sitting with me on my grandmother's sofa while I'm crying into his shoulder. "Sydney, you should never think you can't tell me anything." It was the moment I told him about how all of the name-calling in school was getting to me. "Sydney, we're more than best friends. We are *family*. You are like another sister to me. Know that I'm always going to be here for you. No matter what."

No matter what.

My flashback is broken by recent memories of the fights we've had . . . of the way I felt when I saw him in his tux for the Christmas gala. I miss my friend. Maybe it's time to start letting him in . . . again.

"So, I've been hearing voices."

Corey is quiet. I gulp down the last of my champagne and can only imagine the look he has on his face. I chuckle at the thought of it.

"Humphries, what are you talking about?"

"Not like 'I see dead people' voices. But, you know, a voice."

"Like God? Has he been talking to you?"

"The better question is if she's listening!" Carina yells in the background.

"Tell her I said hello, and I'm fine."

Corey relays the message. "But for real though, you've been hearing God talk to you?"

"At least I think it's him. I don't know. I always feel it and hear it specifically in my left ear—like *deep* within my left ear. I would ask people around me if they've said something. Of course, everyone denies that they did."

"What kinda stuff did you hear?"

"You're filling up on the wrong things. I'm all you need. Stuff like that."

I set my glass down on my coffee table as I make

myself comfortable on the sofa. *Maybe I'll just take today off.* "And you know what I thought about? That time we learned about Samuel in Children's Church."

"Oh yeah?"

"Yeah."

Silence seems to be the third partner in this conversation. I run my fingers through my hair as I put him on speaker phone. It's like we're having to start all over as adults. Like we're meeting each other for the first time yet we've known each other our whole lives.

Incoming calls and texts from Camille come in, but I avoid them. I could use someone else to talk to right now.

Corey and I continue in the small talk phase for a little while. I tell him where I'm living now, all the places I've been to for Fashion Week, Camille … I catch a glimpse of myself in my golden, full-length mirror in the corner of the living room.

I put the phone on the floor as I try to get as full of a view of myself as I can. The size of my legs have gone down. My thighs are half the size they used to be. *My belly is flat though.* My arms are thin, but there's no definition. My diet is all over the place. I barley sleep sometimes, and I barely eat; and when I do, it's sandwiches, fries, or pasta. But then I'm walking or traveling all over the place going from client meeting to client meeting. *But this is my dream, right?*

"I've lost so much weight, bro." *Bro.* That word slipped out so easy. Too easy. "Well, I have to go," I say.

I come to the realization that I won't know the next time I'll hear his voice again. I can't imagine myself trying to call him ... I like hearing his voice.

"Oh, okay. Bye." He clicks off, and I flop onto the sofa, letting out a scream. I throw my shoes across the room as if I'm throwing a pitch on the Phillies' mound. Both shoes bounce off of the window as I put my hands over my face and cry.

"I'm supposed to be happy. Why am I not happy?" I yell to no one. Camille's text and phone calls keep my phone ringing and buzzing for minutes at a time. After a while, I turn off my phone.

"I'm going to take the day off."

CHAPTER SEVENTEEN

MAY 30TH

The last couple of months have been like walking through Dante's inferno. Camille got increasingly annoying and picky and needy; Mr. Barnes vetoed my decision to fire Olivia and rehired her; and Tristan doesn't talk to me at all unless he absolutely has to.

I'm glad I don't have to see any of their faces this morning since I have to get ready for this polo game. My pastel pink strapless dress comes to my shins—a nod to Audrey Hepburn with the silhouette. My grandma would've loved this dress. I pair the dress with white heels and a white leather clutch. Going full Audrey, I slick my hair back into a bun to show pearl earrings that match the pearl necklace

I'm wearing. My phone buzzes, letting me know my driver is downstairs. *Right on time.*

I get into my black Escalade with my shades on and put in my earphones. This ride is in need of a soundtrack.

"Ms. Humphries! We're here, ma'am."

Oh, wow. I didn't even realize I fell asleep. We're in front of a classic, colonial house with large pillars in the entrance. As I walk in, I'm greeted with the familiar hub-bub of conversation, scraping utensils, and popping wine corks. This year's game is at a different location—a larger location.

I step into the front entrance and am greeted with staircases that flank both sides of me like a parenthesis. In the middle of the entrance hall stands a brown, wooden table with a tall vase containing all types of flowers: sunflowers, roses, tulips. The fragrance from the flowers reminds me of what would happen if spring and summer got together to hang out. The floors are marked in black and white tiles with the black tiles creating a larger square pattern throughout the space. People are dipping in and out of various rooms as I make my way further back to the grand receiving room.

Servers in tuxedos offer me trays of food, but what I'm really looking for is—

"Ah, yes. Thank you." I take a glass of pink

champagne off of a tray. Ignoring the fact that the champagne will hit me harder with no food on my stomach. That's the least of my worries. I want to numb myself as much as I can so this day can be over.

I hear a familiar laugh when I turn around to see Olivia coming into the room on Nicholas's arm.

My whole body tenses up. I down the last of the champagne then replace my empty glass with a new one.

Olivia walks right up to me. "Sydney. I see you're doing well." She looks me up and down. "You know Nicholas." She smiles.

If only a laser could shoot out of my eyes like Superman.

Nicholas looks everywhere else but at me. He's still handsome, I have to admit, but that fragrance that was once comforting and sweet is a stench that I wish could be exterminated. One hand is in the pocket of his blue chino pants while Olivia's lanky arm is threaded in between the other.

I envy Superman.

As if things couldn't get worse, I spy a particularly tall gentleman who's wearing a white Oxofrd shirt with sleeves rolled up to his elbows. I grab another drink.

"Hey," Corey says with a soft smile. We decide to hug.

"Hey." I take a sip and look at Carina. "You look nice, Carina."

"Thanks," she says with a smile. "You look nice too."

I look down at my DVF dress and take another sip. *This champagne is really good.*

"What are you guys doing here?" I ask.

"When did you start drinking?" Corey asks with a concerned look on his face.

"Comes with the job," I say with a light chuckle. "Now, tell me, what are you guys doing here?"

"Oh, my foundation is one of the sponsors of the game," Corey says.

"Foundation?"

"Yeah, I started a sports foundation for kids to give them an alternative from being on the street."

Of course, he started a foundation! I nod and chuckle as I begin to feel the bubbly of the champagne make its way to my system.

"Sydney, are you okay?"

"I'm fine," I say. I guess I was a little too loud because Carina looks to either side of her.

I walk over to the bar, stumbling a bit at first, but I get my bearings. Holding myself up on the counter, I ask the bartender for food.

"I don't have food ma'am. There are servers walking around with trays of food."

"I want food now!" The words come slower out of

my mouth then what they feel like in my head. Out of the corner of my right eye, I see Olivia take out her phone.

"Where is a server!" I yell. The floor gets closer and closer in view as I feel Corey come behind me to lift me up. "What is going on? Why are you here?"

"C'mon, I think you've had one too many."

"What do you mean one too many? One can *never* have too many glasses of champagne, darling." The thought of my horrible British accent makes me chuckle uncontrollably. "Hey, turn that camera off, you witch." I say to Olivia. I try to swipe her phone, but I end up falling face-first on the ground.

Carina and Corey come on either side of me, each wrapping one of my arms around their necks, and head toward the front door.

"But I don't wanna leave!" I whine. Their grip gets harder as I try to pull away from them. "Let me go! Let me go!" I continue to scream. Kicking, pushing, screaming, I'm going to do whatever I have to do to stay here. They *need* me here.

"Get off of me!" I'm on the circular driveway as I look at Carina and Corey and notice Nicholas and Olivia standing on the steps.

Olivia still has her blasted phone out.

I scream out a curse as I turn around and walk. Where to? I have no clue, but I'm going somewhere.

"I'm living my dream! I should be on top of the world!" I yell to the sky. *How long is this driveway?*

"Sydney, wait!"

That's the last thing I hear as I walk toward the street to find a taxi getting closer. I begin to run further out into the street when suddenly my bright world goes dark.

CHAPTER EIGHTEEN

MAY 31ST

A series of beeps wake me up to a bunch of bright lights and a headache the size of Texas.

"Where am I?"

Corey and Carina are on either side of me, looking at me laying in this hospital bed. *Hospital bed? Why am I in the hospital?* I sit up more abruptly only to be taken down my headache.

"Easy. Easy." Corey says. "How are you feeling?"

"My throat feels like I swallowed a truck."

Carina pats my hand and smiles. "I'm glad you're feeling a little better." She slaps my hand with a resounding sting. "Now, don't you ever do that again, you hear me? Don't you ever put us through that again."

"What happened?"

"You collided with a moving car in the middle of the street."

"What?"

"I was trying to catch up with you, but I was too late. A car was trying to swerve out of the way," Corey says, "but you were stumbling in every direction. The driver is in the waiting room."

I close my eyes and lean my head back on the pillow. A wave of embarrassment, shame, and guilt wash over my entire body. The last thing I remember is Olivia and Nicholas standing arm in arm in a beautiful house. My stomach rumbles as deep as an earthquake.

"Is there any good food I can have right now?" I ask

"Carina and I will pick you up something. You rest up. Go back to sleep. We'll be right back."

Through the slit of my eyelashes, I see Carina and Corey walk out of the room. I close my eyes fully and allow my head to sink deeper into the pillow.

I'm right here. I've always been here. I'll never leave you.

I slowly open my eyes and let out a sigh when I see the same empty room I saw moments before. I take a few deep breaths.

"Alright, God. I'm here. I don't have anywhere else to go. Nothing to do."

Why have you been running away from me?

"I haven't been running away from you." I take a few slow breaths. *Right?*

Why have you been running away from me?

I close my eyes and feel the well of tears begin to bubble over.

"Why did you have to make me this way? Why couldn't you give me parents that are alive? Why did I have to grow up poor? Why couldn't I get that job after college? My life sucks."

Daughter, if you were to get planted in the church that I have set you in, you would find that you have all the family you need. I've provided you with a mother and father through the pastor and his wife. I've giving you siblings through Carina and Corey. Your finances were taken care of through your position at the café. I am the one who brings increase and promotion. But it has to be done in my timing.

"God, I just wanted my life to be different. I just wanted my life to count for something." I close my eyes and feel the memories of taunts, fights, objects being thrown ... "I just wanted my life to be different," I mutter under tear-stained cheeks. "I just want it all to go away. I want all of the memories to go away."

Daughter, know that I was with you then, and I am with you now. I have always been with you.

I feel a hand on my shoulder.

"I just wanted my life to be different. I just wanted to write my own story."

Corey wraps his arms around me as my shoulders

begin to shake up and down sparking a deeper cry to come from my soul. All of my heartaches, all of my brokenness, it comes to the surface…like when all of the impurities come to the top as you're purifying gold in a fire. I've buried my pain for so long that I never actually dealt with it. I never talked with Corey and Carina about it or even a pastor at my church.

My church.

I never talked to God about it. Instead, I blamed Him for it.

And even through all of it, God never left me. You could even say he *refused* to leave me. He was there through the taunts, the bullying, the death, the low self-esteem. I just didn't notice it—or maybe I didn't *want* to notice it. My heart had been trampled upon so many times that I decided to take matters into my own hands. I became Creator and decided to form and fashion my life in the way that I thought was best. As long as I had control, no one would ever hurt me again. With the right wardrobe, no one could talk about me again. Being the perfect size and weight, I could have any guy that I wanted…and life would finally be worth living.

But then again, what *is* the meaning of life?

CHAPTER NINETEEN

JULY 1ST

I was in the hospital for about a week before I was sent home, and even at home, I got kicked out because of the mess and noise I constantly made during my massive drinking spells.

Thankfully, Carina allowed me to move back in with her. Mr. Barnes caught wind of my antics at the polo game and swiftly let me go. Now I'm back to square one. All of the contacts I made during Fashion Week are useless; no one answers my calls or emails. They can't seem to separate my work from what I did at the polo game.

God and I had a few more conversations since the one in the hospital room. I downloaded the Bible app on my phone and have been reading a few verses every now and then. Deciding to go to church with Corey and Carina was a hard one, but I'm curious as to the life God has for me. If I do things his way, maybe it will turn out better. I guess I'll have to see.

* * *

After service, Corey, Carina, and I go to Olive Garden for lunch.

"It's good to have you back, Syd. I missed you," Carina said after we put in our orders.

"I can't lie and say that it's good to be back. I miss my apartment so much."

"Yeah, well, that was your own fault," Carina says as she rubs my back.

"But you don't understand, I've now had a taste of that life, and to not have it anymore . . ." I let out a big sigh. "This is going to be difficult." I move out of the booth so Carina could go to the restroom, leaving Corey and me across from each other.

"It's been good to have you back," he says with a smile.

"I've missed you guys. There were so many times I wanted to call you guys when something happened, but I couldn't bring myself to do it."

"Why not?" He leans his back against the booth.

I look at him and shake my head.

"C'mon," he says, "tell me. You can say it."

I take a deep breath in.

"I still wanted to feel like I had everything under control. I couldn't stand to tell you that everything was going bad after all the times I fought you about it."

"But you know what? Carina and I were talking, and we could see where we were wrong. It was as if we threw your cares to the side and only wanted you to care about us. You've always been our biggest supporter, and we love you for that. But when it was time to support you, we didn't know how to do it. We were so used to you always being there for us that we didn't realize that it needs to go both ways."

I twiddle with my thumbs and smile. Corey's curly hair is just below his ears now. I'm glad he decided to grow his hair out. He looks handsome with his hair that length. *Ew, what am I saying?*

"What's wrong?"

Oh great, my inner thoughts are showing on my face.

"Uh, nothing."

"You know, I was thinking," he says as he drums his fingers on the table. "You owe me a week's worth of meals from the Christmas gala a couple of years ago."

"Excuse me?" I say playfully, holding my hand to my chest.

"I won the bet fair and square. I never complained. You owe me food."

"I can pay for your meal today."

"Nope. That wasn't a part of the deal."

We smile at each other, and for some reason my reflex is to look at the table. My cheeks get warm as I take a sip of water.

"You know I hate cooking," I say looking at him.

"I know."

We hold each other's gaze.

"I *know* you, Sydney. And I want you to know that I'll always be here."

He grabs my hand and I can feel my eyes begin to well up with tears. Corey *has* been there. My fingers relax onto the top of his hand as I look at him and smile and take another sip of water.

"Corey, how come you haven't had a girlfriend?"

I immediately put my hands over my mouth and regret every second that just went by. My shoulders sag in defeat as I look into my water glass. One of these days my inside thoughts will remain inside.

"Truth?" he responds.

Welp, might as well lay in the bed I just made.

"Truth," I say taking a sip of water.

"I've been going back and forth with how to tell you how I feel about you."

Water spews out of my mouth like Old Faithful the geyser, and I rush to grab any and all napkins that I can find at our table. My heart is beating at an accelerated rate as sweat beads form around my hairline.

"Umm, feelings?" I respond.

"Syd, I've had feelings for you for a *long* time. I

just didn't know when was the right time to talk to you about them. And then there was the Christmas gala—"

The Christmas gala?

"I was going to tell you that evening once we left the event."

That's why he wanted to leave early?

The spit landing on my hand let me know that my mouth had been open.

"Sydney...what do you think about what I just said?"

"Uh..."

Corey's gray eyes look at me with such hope, warmth, and love.

"I...I...I honestly don't know what to say."

He puts his head down, still holding my hand and looks back up at me.

"Say that you'll have dinner with me, just the two of us. We can even go to one of those fancy restaurants if you want to."

A smile forms on my face,

My best friend. He is my best friend.

"I would like that a lot."

"Besides, you owe me a week's worth of meals from our bet, and you'll definitely be needing food once you burn down the kitchen," he says

I ball up a napkin and throw it at him as he laughs.

"What's so funny?" Carina says as I get up to let her back into the booth.

"Imagine Sydney trying to cook in a kitchen."

"Oh my gosh, no!" Carina says emphatically while taking a sip of her lemonade.

"Hey now—" and the vibrancy of all of the conversations comes flooding back in that moment as we playfully make fun of each other.

You're right God, these two are my family.

All I ever needed or wanted was right here this whole time.

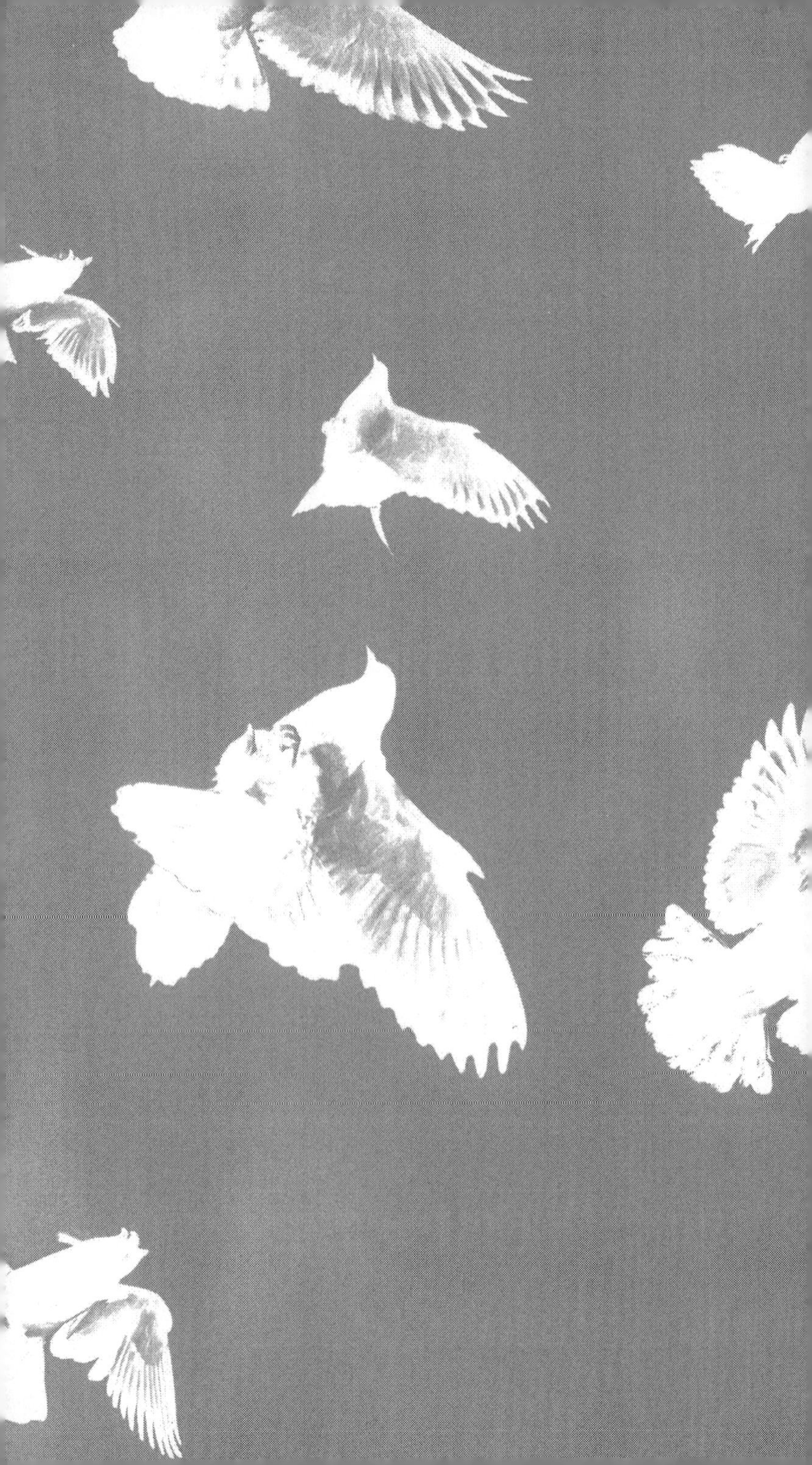

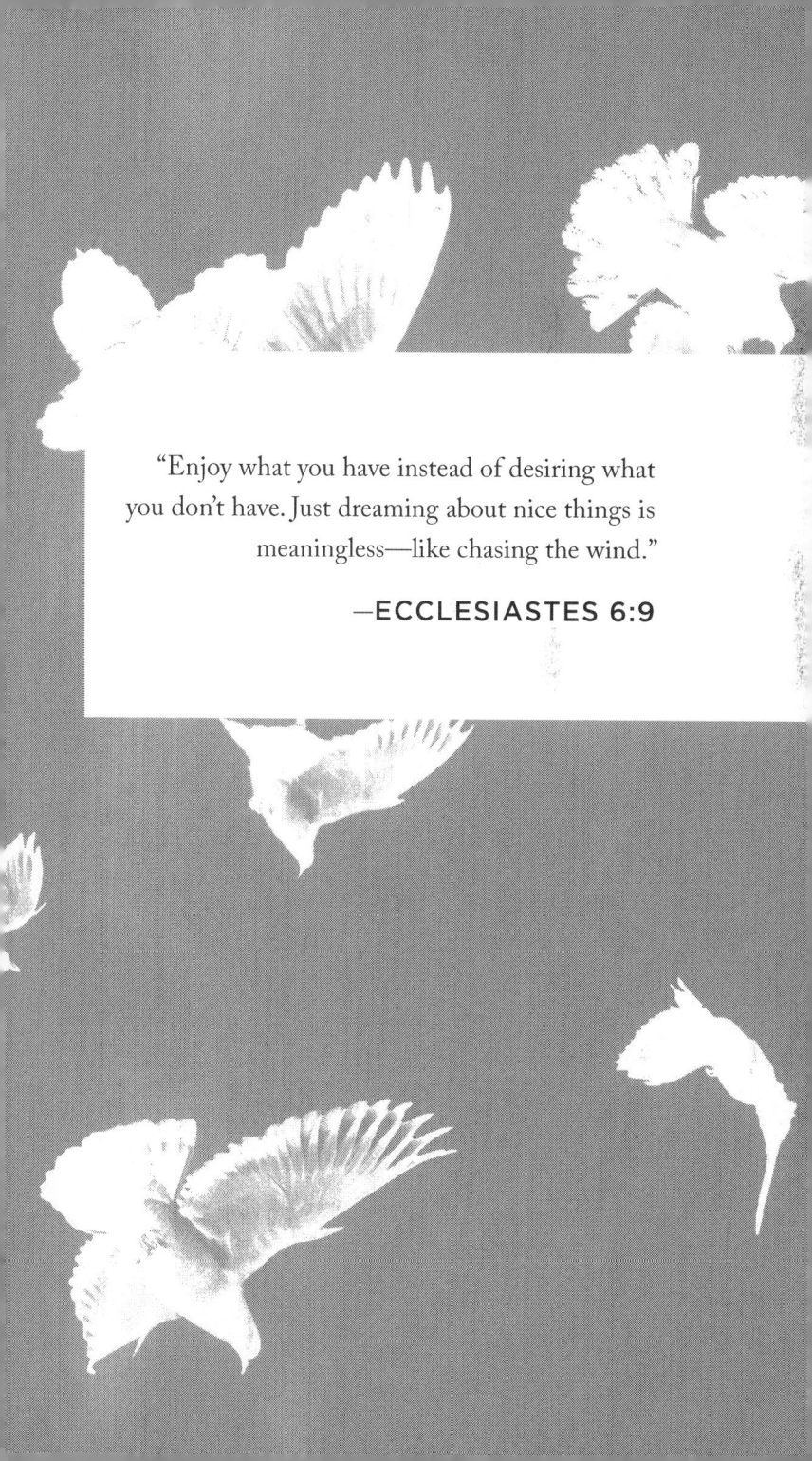

"Enjoy what you have instead of desiring what you don't have. Just dreaming about nice things is meaningless—like chasing the wind."

—ECCLESIASTES 6:9

ACKNOWLEDGEMENTS

I first want to thank the greatest creator of all, God, for your patience, mercy, faithfulness, and creativity as I brought Sydney's story to life.

Dad: thank you so much for always believing in me and supporting me through every life transition.

Mom: my biggest supporter, I love you to the moon and back. Pack a bag! It's time to celebrate!

My sister, Ayanna: You're my dance partner, freestyle partner, and overall turn-up partner (you're probably smiling right now as you're reading this aren't you?). Thank you for always keeping me on my toes and keeping me in line when I feel like quitting. I love you my little cactus (HA!).

To Pastor Vincent J. Stevens and Apostle Stephanie Stevens, who I grew up calling Uncle Tiba and Aunt Niambi: wow, wow, wow. I've been waiting for the day where I could get this book into your hands and it's finally here. Thank you so much for always pushing me. You always saw greater in me than what I saw in myself, and you would not stop until I reached it (and you still aren't stopping because there's more to be done). Thank you for reminding me of what's important and *who's* important.

To Onaje, Njeri, and Tia: My cousins! I love you guys beyond words (yikes, the tears are starting to form as I'm writing this at 4:47 in the morning). Thank you so much for adopting me as your sister. Through the good, the bad, and the devastatingly ugly, you guys have always remained my family. I want to share this moment with you and shout at the top of my lungs, "We did it!"

To my church, Harvest Time Christian Fellowship: I've always wanted a big family, and I'm grateful God answered my unspoken prayer through you.

To Ann Shafer, Gabrielle Graf-Palmer, Anita Fuller, Stella Fairly, and Katrina Hartwell: your support of me and for this book is deeply felt. I appreciate all of your thoughts, prayers, and contributions towards getting this book published.

To the reader: thank you so much for going on this journey with me. Whether we have a personal connection, or you were just intrigued by the synopsis, I appreciate you taking the time to immerse yourself into the world of Sydney Humphries.

May the imagination of the modern-day consumer be awakened to God as Creator.

ABOUT THE AUTHOR

As a Christmas enthusiast and self-proclaimed Narnian, **Dara Alston** holds a bachelor's degree in English and a master's degree in Interior Architecture. She has started her own print and digital media company, Avenue 89 Co, which is the parent company (or as she likes to call it "the creative warehouse") of Inkwell Publishing. Avenue 89 Co is also home to Studio 89: her podcast network where she hosts the following podcasts: *The Book Sail* (all about literature), *Dear Hallmark* (all about the Hallmark Channel), and *The 89th Record* (a music podcast co-hosted with Atiba Halisi). She's currently enjoying daily visits to her imagination to see what new worlds she can create.

To learn more about Avenue 89 Co, visit ave89co.com

Connect with Dara:
Email: dara@ave89co.com
Instagram: @astoldbydara

Made in the USA
Middletown, DE
14 September 2024